BEN'S DEN

BEN'S DEN

EDWARD TERRELL SR.

TATE PUBLISHING
AND ENTERPRISES, LLC

Published by Tate Publishing & Enterprises, LLC
127 E. Trade Center Terrace | Mustang, Oklahoma 73064 USA
1.888.361.9473 | www.tatepublishing.com

Tate Publishing is committed to excellence in the publishing industry. The company reflects the philosophy established by the founders, based on Psalm 68:11,
"The Lord gave the word and great was the company of those who published it."

Book design copyright © 2012 by Tate Publishing, LLC. All rights reserved.
Cover design by Erin DeMoss
Interior design by Nathan Harmony

Published in the United States of America

ISBN: 978-1-61862-157-3
Fiction / Coming Of Age
12.01.12

DEDICATION

Right before the production of Ben's Den began, my family was very unfortunate to lose my nephew. He was my sister's miracle baby and meant a lot to the whole family. Nathaniel Allen Terrell was this amazing little man's name, and he was involved in a accidental shooting, just like in *Ben's Den*. I want the world to know the importance of gun safety, and parents, even if you don't believe in owning firearms, the fact still remains that teenagers are going to get their hands on anything they want. Please teach the safety and importance of leaving firearms alone or teaching them the safe way to use them. If this dedication leads to even saving ten lives then I hope this would not let my nephew's death be in vain. Words can not explain the way you feel when you lose someone who is like your son, and I hope any of you that read my book never have to feel that pain. Nathaniel was a little man full of life and his ended too soon. Please take this to heart.

Nathaniel Allen Terrell
a.k.a.
"Texas"

Blessed the world on the day of February 19, 1995 and left this world a little dimmer on the day of June 19, 2011.

Rest in peace nephew knowing that you were loved more than this world.

Loved always and forever.

SOFTNESS OF A TEAR

I felt the softness of a tear,
when I lost my nephew I loved so dear,
the fear of death we try to ignore,
sooner or later it knocks at life's door,
in our lives no matter what we do,
this I know will always be true,
when you lose a loved one you love dear,
you too will feel the softness of a tear.

TABLE OF CONTENTS

MISTER RIGHT

"Hey, Lauren, you coming or not?" yelled Jessica.

"Yeah, I am almost ready," Lauren replied.

"Okay. I'll be in the car," Jessica told Lauren as she shut the door to their dorm room.

Lauren Worth was in her third year of college, and the tension of finding a good man was building inside of her. She stood in front of her bathroom mirror wandering what was wrong with her.

My hair must be messed up at all the wrong moments, she thought to herself. *Will this be the night I meet mister right, or am I getting my hopes up again?*

Lauren knew these college parties were not the best place to find mister right, but in this small college town, she did not have much choice. Lauren was a very timid girl and was not as spontaneous as the other girls she palled around with. Most guys were more likely to go for girls like Jessica. They had better odds of getting laid and did not have to worry about strings being attached. Lauren was not the type to go sleeping around with guys she barely knew. Lauren was old fashioned; she had very high morals and liked the fact that it made her different from the other girls. Lauren came from a small farm town in Kansas where everyone knew everyone, so doing something that might tarnish her family name was not allowed by her father.

Well, I do not want to keep them waiting, so I better get down to the car, she told herself. Lauren made her way down to the car where the other girls were waiting on her.

Jessica came from a wealthy family that made their money from a big oil strike in the seventies. The girls were headed to the party in Jessica's BMW, and when they pulled up, the party was jumping.

"Let's go party, baby!" yelled Jessica.

Jessica was a very flamboyant person—always ready for adventure. She was always getting Lauren to do things she did not think she could do. The previous summer, they'd gone skydiving together, and Jessica had had to pull Lauren onto the plane. Jessica gave her a pep talk on the way up, and when it came time to jump, Lauren watched Jessica heave herself out of the plane. Lauren then decided, *If she can do it, then I can do it.* Those were the kinds of things that made Lauren happy they were friends.

Parties were not Lauren's thing, but she did not want people to think she was an outcast, either.

"Hey, Lauren!" yelled Molly Pops. Molly was probably the prettiest girl in college, and everyone loved her.

"What's up, Molly?" Jessica asked.

"Nothing but this awesome party," Molly replied.

"Yeah; whose house is this?" Lauren asked.

"This is Bob Trestle's house. His dad is the richest man in the county."

Molly jumped as Bob grabbed her waist, picking her up and yelling, "It's party time, people!"

Lauren was almost drenched in beer; when Molly was lifted, her beer flew everywhere. Molly was getting carried away when she turned her head back and said, "Follow us. The beer is this way, girls."

Lauren and Jessica followed. The corridor was starting to get packed with students who were ready to party. Jessica made her way to the big kitchen as Lauren headed for cover. Lauren eased her way into a front living room where there was, to her surprise, one guy sitting. "I'm sorry, am I intruding?" she asked.

The man got up and turned toward Lauren.

"No," he said. Their eyes locked for a brief moment. "Hey, I'm going to let you go, Bill. I'll call you tomorrow." He hung up his phone. "What I *meant* to say was that there's no way a beautiful women like you could ever be intruding."

Lauren's face blushed as she inched her way into the room.

"My name is Lauren. What's yours?" she asked.

"Frank." He paused. "Frank Cassel." Frank thought to himself that he had never seen such beauty in his life.

Lauren was about five foot five, had shiny brown hair, and was very petite. Frank was six foot one and a little on the heavy side. Frank worried about his appearance a lot, which hindered his ability to hit on women most of the time. There was something different about Lauren, though. When she walked into the room, he got a feeling of ease from her unlike any he had ever gotten before.

"Why is a pretty girl like you not out with the rest of the party?" he asked.

"I'm not really much for parties. I just go out to shut my friends up," she replied.

"That's funny—I'm not really into the whole party thing either. I could go for a movie and popcorn. That seems like more fun to me," Frank said with a big grin.

Lauren thought to herself, *This guy is too good to be true. I love a good movie and popcorn and like good company to go along with it.* Lauren then got the nerve to ask Frank if he wanted to leave the party to go back to her dorm.

"I've got a couple of good movies back at my dorm room if you want to join me," she said.

"Sure, that sounds like a good time. Did you drive to the party?" he asked.

"No, I don't have a car," she told him.

"Well, I do. Let's get out of here," he replied. That is exactly what they did; no one even realized they had left. They went straight out to Frank's truck and headed for the dorms.

"So, what are you going to college for, Frank?" asked Lauren.

"Business management," he replied. "My Uncle is going to turn the family business over to me eventually—with the stipulation that I go to college for business management. So, here I am," Frank told her.

"That sounds like a pretty good deal, Frank," she said.

"So, what are you going for?" asked Frank.

"I want to be a teacher," she replied.

"That is honorable," he said.

The radio station on campus had just played Lynard Skynard's "Sweet Home Alabama." They both jammed out to the music the rest of the way to the dorm. When they arrived at the dorm, Lauren was second-guessing her decision to invite him. She then turned her head, and they locked eyes. Gazing into his green eyes, she realized that, for the first time in her life, this felt right. There was no uneasy feeling in her stomach like she had gotten many times before.

"So, you ready to go up?" Lauren asked.

"I will follow you," Frank replied.

They went up to the room and got the popcorn ready for the movie. Frank noticed that there was no couch or anything—just two beds. Right at that moment, Lauren screamed.

"Oh my gosh!" she cried.

"What is it?" Frank asked with a look of panic.

"There is a big black bug on my bathroom sink!" she said. She was hyperventilating.

Frank gently nudged her to the side, slipped off his shoe, and smashed the bug.

"There you go. 'Nothing to be afraid of now," Frank said.

"Thank you," she said, laughing.

"What?" he asked.

"I probably scared you half to death," she said.

"No, it was closer to a quarter to death," he replied.

They both started laughing hysterically, and then engaged in a staring contest. Lauren thought to herself, *He'll go for it*. She then lunged forward, locking lips with Frank.

It lasted about a minute, and when it was over, they both had fireworks in their eyes and butterflies in their stomachs. After they were done kissing, they settled down on Lauren's bed to watch the movie. For the first time, Lauren felt comfortable in a man's arms. Frank was also thinking to himself how comfortable it felt holding Lauren in his arms. They both fell asleep in this position and the night came to a wonderful end.

Lauren and Frank both knew that the night they had shared was something special, and from that moment every chance they had, they were together. It was about four months later when Frank popped the big question. A year and half later, Frank and Lauren were ringing wedding bells.

"Let's run for it, Lauren," Frank said. "I think we can make it to the limo," he added as they laughed.

They were standing just inside the doorway of the local Methodist Church in Frank's hometown. As they took off running, they started to get smashed with water balloons. This was the great idea of Frank's fraternity brothers. Frank and Lauren made it to the limo and slid inside, both laughing their faces off.

"This is the happiest day of my life, Frank. I love you," said Lauren.

"I love you too, baby. 'You ready for the honeymoon surprise?" Frank asked.

"Of course! Where are we headed?" she asked.

"I can't tell you, or it wouldn't be a surprise," he said with a big smile.

Frank's uncle Kirk had purchased them a three-night stay at the Mirage Hotel in Las Vegas. Frank was keeping it a secret so that he could surprise Lauren; she had never been to Vegas.

They got to the airport and the flight was right on schedule. They boarded the plane with no problems and were on their way to Vegas. Frank had dozed off thirty minutes before the plane was scheduled to land. Lauren could see the lights of Vegas and was excited about this surprise. The seatbelt sign came on, so Lauren reached over and unbuckled Frank's seatbelt for him. He was still asleep when Lauren started to shake him.

"*Mayday, Mayday, Mayday*! We're going down!" she yelled.

Frank jumped up in a panic.

"*What do we do?*" he screamed.

Just then, he realized that the plane was at a stop already and that people were calmly getting off.

"Hahaha." Lauren was laughing uncontrollably.

"You're going to get it!" Frank said as he started to chase her down the aisle of the plane.

When they got to the exit, the pilot was coming out of the cockpit.

"Don't worry. We are on our honeymoon," Frank said.

The pilot just looked at them with a wondering eye and then began to laugh.

"Let's get out to a cab, baby, so we can get to our hotel," Frank said.

"Let's, honey. I have a big night planned," Lauren replied.

As they were riding in the cab to the hotel, Lauren was amazed by the lights of Vegas. She had never seen such a thing in her life; she had seen it on TV, but this was the first time she had seen them in person. When they arrived to the hotel, Frank went to check in at the front desk and Lauren waited in the lobby. *The hotel is beautiful*, she thought to herself. *This is going to be a memorable time.*

"Room 406 is where we are going, Lauren," Frank said.

"Well, let's get to going then, baby," she replied. "Why are you walking so fast, Frank?" she asked.

"I'm ready for what is coming," he said with a big grin.

"I am ready, too, sweetie, but that room isn't going anywhere. Besides, my legs are killing me," she said.

They made it to the elevator and were alone when they got on it. Lauren grabbed Frank when the door shut and they started making out. The elevator had stopped on the third floor when an elderly couple got on. They knew what Frank and Lauren had been doing.

"'Did you guys just get married?" the elderly man asked.

"'Sure did. 'On our honeymoon," Frank replied.

"I can see the fire in your eyes. It reminds me of us forty years ago," the elderly man told them.

"Forty years? Congratulations," Lauren said.

"Well, this is our floor. You guys have a good day," Frank said.

"Best of wishes to you newlyweds," the elderly man replied.

"Thank you," they said as they got off the elevator.

"The honeymoon suite! I cannot believe Uncle Kirk went and got us the *suite*," Frank said.

"I know. That was *sweet* of him," Lauren replied. as they both started laughing about the words sweet and suite.

They made it to the room, and Lauren's jaw had dropped as they walked through the door. She had never seen such a beautiful hotel room in person; she had only seen pictures in magazines. "I am going to get freshened up," Lauren said.

"Alright, I'll be here waiting on you," Frank replied.

Frank was ready to make love to his wife, and knew she felt the same way. As she came out of the bathroom, Frank was starting to drool on himself.

"Wow," he said with excitement.

Lauren had on a white lace teddy and high heels. "You want this, baby?" she asked in a sexy, soothing voice.

They embraced, and the sparks were flying. They both knew this would be a night that neither one of them would forget. What they did not know was that the night would bring a lot more than memories in nine months.

IT'S A BOY

Four months had passed. Frank and Lauren were staying with Frank's uncle Kirk for the time being. Kirk was fifty-five and was not in very good shape. Frank's dad had passed away when Frank was only twelve. Uncle Kirk had stepped in and helped his mom raise Frank. When Frank was fifteen, his mom got into a bad car accident, and she did not survive the wreck. Kirk had finished raising Frank on his own. Kirk paid Frank's way through college so that he could take over the heating and air conditioning business that Kirk and Frank's dad had started when they were in their late twenties. With his health fading, Kirk knew it was time to turn the reins over to Frank.

Frank was going to stay with Kirk until he had saved up enough money for a down payment on a house. Frank and Lauren decided that they were going to get a house nearby so that they could be there for Kirk. Frank had explained to Lauren already the way Kirk had always been there for him. Frank was going to return the favor, since Kirk was the only family they had left. Lauren respected Frank for what he had planned and was backing him one hundred percent.

Kirk had Parkinson's disease, and some days were better than others. Kirk had drunk a lot of beer when he was younger to help calm his shakes from the disease. All that drinking had caught up with him in the past few years and taken a toll on his liver. Kirk's doctor had told him that he would have to quit drinking if he did not want to die earlier than expected. Kirk realized he wanted to be around when Frank's kid was born and took the doctor's advice. Marriage never occurred in Kirk's life, so he had no biological kids of his own. He always thought of Frank as his own after Frank's parents passed. Kirk was always looking out for Frank, and even offered to put a down payment on a house for Frank and Lauren. Frank told him that he would save up his own money and earn it on his own. Kirk was a stubborn man, but when it came to Frank, he would give Frank his way.

It was May 14, 1986, and the day had come for the baby to make its way into the world.

"*Uncle Kirk!*" Lauren yelled. "My water just broke. It's time, call Frank!" she added.

"I'm on it, Lauren," Kirk yelled back.

Frank was at the office working when he got the call. "Cassel Heating and Air, Frank speaking."

"Frank, it's your uncle. Lauren's water broke!" Kirk said in a panic.

Frank jumped so high that he fell backward in his chair. The phone had fallen under the desk, and Frank was on the floor. He could hear, "Frank? Frank—?" coming from the phone.

Frank scurried over and grabbed the phone. "Uncle Kirk, can you get her to the hospital?" he asked.

"I think so," Kirk replied.

"There's a suitcase in our closet. It is packed and ready to go. Grab it and get Lauren to the hospital. I will meet you guys there," Frank told Kirk.

"Okay, Frank," Kirk replied.

Frank had tried to hurry but got caught up by a train delay, and then a traffic accident which delayed him about an hour.

When Frank got to the hospital, Lauren had already been rushed up to the delivery room about fifty minutes prior to then.

"My name is Frank Cassel, and my wife is in labor," he told the nurse at the front desk.

"One minute, sir," the nurse replied. She then turned to look at a sheet of paper on the wall.

"Your wife is in delivery room twenty-one. Go all the way down the hall and the room will be on the right-hand side," the nurse told him.

"Thank you," he replied. Frank hurried down the hall telling himself, this is it; he could not believe the day was already here. Frank opened the door to the room, and Lauren was grunting.

"Oh, Frank, *come here*!" Lauren squealed. "This hurts, Frank," she added.

"Everything is going to be all right, baby," Frank told her in a reassuring voice.

"Are you sure, Frank?" she asked.

"Yes, honey, just keep pushing and it will all be over soon," he said. Frank then embraced her and kissed her on the forehead. "I love you," Frank told her.

"I love you, too, Frank," she replied in a high-pitched voice.

Just then, they heard the cry of their baby for the first time.

"It's a boy!" the doctor said.

"A boy? Did you hear that, honey? You gave me a boy!" Frank said with tears of joy coming down his face.

"It was all worth it," Lauren said with a smile. Lauren was worn out and needed to rest.

Frank stood there with his newborn son, looking down on Lauren. "I think you look like a *Ben* to me. We will ask Mama what she thinks when she wakes up," Frank told the baby. Frank sat in the recliner next to the bed. He held his son, waiting in anticipation for Lauren to wake up.

THE BIG MOVE

Four years went by in the blink of an eye. Ben's parents delayed getting a house, because they were waiting for the right one. A big house went up for sale the month Ben turned four years old. Ben's parents were excited about the house—especially his dad. His dad liked the fact that they were only a few blocks from Uncle Kirk. Frank put the down payment on it and it was theirs.

As they were moving in, the neighbors decided to introduce themselves. "Hi, my name is Jack Henson. This is my wife, Darlene, and my daughter, Stephanie," the man said.

Ben's parents then introduced themselves and before they could tell them Ben's name. "My name is Ben," he said, giggling. Ben kept looking over at Stephanie and smiling the whole time they were talking.

"I think someone has gotten his first crush," said Ben's mom.

"I think you're right," Darlene replied.

"How old is Ben?" asked Jack.

"He turned four just last month," Ben's mom said as she rubbed Ben's brown hair.

"You're a big boy. 'You going to play football, Ben?" asked Jack.

"I like soccer ball." Ben replied.

They all started laughing, and Stephanie had something to say, also. "I like soccer ball, too," she said.

"Well, I think these two should get along just swell," Ben's dad said.

"Yeah, Stephanie turned four just last March, so they are the same age," Darlene told them.

"Well, after we get settled in, I can bring Ben over to ask Stephanie if she wants to play," Ben's mom said.

"That sounds great. We'll see you guys later," Jack said.

"Bye," Ben said with a big smile on his face.

"Bye-bye!" Stephanie replied as she smiled back, holding her dad's hand.

"They seem like nice people," Ben's mom said.

"Yeah, they do, don't they? I think someone is going to have a little girlfriend," his dad replied.

The house had tall ceilings and nice hardwood floors that Ben could slide across with his socks on. They took Ben up to his room so he could see what they had put in there for him. When they opened the door, the first thing Ben could see was his racecar bed.

"*Racecar bed!*" Ben yelled. "*Alright!* I *love* racecars, Mom!" he said as he ran over and jumped on his bed.

"Good, because we've got another surprise," she said as she watched his eyes light up.

"Another suupise?" Ben said as he pronounced surprise wrong.

"Yeah, come with me buddy," his dad said.

They made their way to the backyard, which was not all that big, but was layered in beautiful Bermuda grass. The back patio doors were French doors that opened up to a nice deck. Ben's dad barely got them open before Ben came barging through.

"Wow, Daddy, a *wingset*," Ben said in amazement.

Ben could speak pretty well for four-year-old, but some words he was still a little confused by, and "swing set" was one of them. The swing set was one of those big wood ones with a deck on one side and a slide coming off of it. Swings were tied into it and took up the other side.

"Can I climb the ladder, Dad?" Ben asked.

"Sure, son, go for it," his dad said as they raced for the ladder. "I'll stay behind you, Ben, in case you lose your balance," his dad said.

"'Kay, Dad," Ben replied.

Ben had a serious look of determination as he climbed the ladder. When he got to the top, he looked around like he was on top of the world.

"I see people yards, Dad," Ben said with enjoyment.

"Yeah, you can see people's backyards, Ben," his dad replied. Ben's dad had climbed to the top with Ben. He was getting a thrill out of watching Ben's face and his amazement at being able to see people in their yards. It was the middle of June, and people were out mowing their yards. The house straight behind theirs belonged to a widowed woman who had one son.

"Who's *dat*, Dad?" Ben asked.

"I do not know, son. I guess we can always go find out," his dad replied.

"Let's go, Dad," Ben said.

"Alright, Ben, go down the slide, and I will follow you. Then we will go introduce ourselves," his dad said.

"Alright," Ben replied. Ben shot down the slide to the bottom. Ben's dad then squeezed his butt onto the slide and scooted his way to the bottom. Ben was laughing at his dad as he made his way down.

"You too big for that slide, Dad," he said.

"Yeah, I think your right, Ben," his dad replied.

They made their way to the back gate. All of the fences were privacy fences in that neighborhood; between the fences were alleys. Ben's dad put his hands at the top of the neighbor's fence and lifted himself up.

"Hi there. My name is Frank. My son saw your son and wanted to come over and meet him," his dad said.

"We will be right there," the lady said as she waived her son over. She unlatched her gate and opened it up so they could see each other better.

"Hi there, cutie. What is your name?" she asked Ben.

"My name is Ben," he replied.

"How old are you, Ben?" she then asked.

"I *this* many," he said as he held three fingers up.

"No, Ben, you're *four*. You need to put another finger up," his dad said, laughing.

"My name is Gloria Flores, and this is my son, Jake," she said.

"Hi, Ben. You want to see my dog?" Jake asked.

"Can I, Dad?" Ben then asked his dad.

"Sure. You can step in for a minute," his dad replied. Ben loved animals; his dad pondered the thought of getting Ben his own dog. "So, is there a Mr. Flores, Gloria?" Ben's dad asked.

"There was until last year—he passed away from a heart attack," she told him.

"I am sorry to hear that," he replied. "Well, my wife is in the house unpacking stuff and telling the movers where everything goes. I will have her come out and meet you sometime," he told her.

"'Sounds good," she said.

"Frank? Ben? 'Where are you guys at?" yelled Ben's mom.

"We are back here!" his dad replied.

"'You guys ready to go eat? Your uncle is taking us out to dinner, remember?" she asked.

"Yeah, be there in a minute," his dad answered.

"Tell Jake 'bye,' Ben, we've got to go," his dad told him.

"Bye, Jake. I like your dog!" Ben said.

"You come see us, Ben. You're welcome anytime, and if you guys are free next Saturday afternoon, you're welcome to come to Jake's fifth birthday party," Gloria told them.

"I think we will put it on our agenda," his dad replied.

"What's *agenda* dad?" Ben asked as his dad and Gloria started laughing.

"It just means we will go to the party, son," he replied.

"Cool!" Ben said as he ran back to their yard.

"Nice meeting you, Gloria," Ben's dad said.

"It was good meeting you, too," she replied.

A couple days went by, and Ben's mom finished getting all their things put away.

Ben's dad was at the office working, and Ben was getting stir crazy. "Mom, I bored," Ben said.

"You want to go see if Stephanie is home?" she asked.

"Yeah, Mom, can we? Can we?" Ben said with excitement.

"Yeah, Ben. Let me use the bathroom, and we will go," his mom said.

"'Kay, Mom," Ben replied.

Ben and his mom went out their front door and started walking toward Stephanie's house. They were half way there when they heard a voice coming from between the houses. It was Darlene; she was standing by the side of her house.

"Hey guys, what are you doing?" Darlene asked.

"Ben was getting bored, and I could use a break from unpacking," Ben's mom replied.

"Well, come in the back with me. I just got Stephanie's little pool set up for her. Ben is welcome to swim if it is alright with you." Darlene told his mom.

"Swimming! I like to swim, Mom," Ben said.

"We will have to go get your trunks on, Ben," his mom told him.

"Just come on into the back when you guys are ready," Darlene said.

About fifteen minutes later, Ben and his mom came through the Henson's back gate.

"Hi, Ben. I swimming!" Stephanie said while she splashed her arms in the pool. The pool was only a couple of feet deep—just big enough for the little ones to get wet.

"Go for it, Ben," his mom told him.

Ben was not shy; he reared his little arms back and took off running for the pool. When he was about a foot away, he threw his little body into the pool.

"*Ben!*" his mom said with disbelief on her face.

"He is alright. Stephanie does it all the time," Darlene told her. "Will you keep an eye on Stephanie? I will go get us some lemonade," Darlene said.

"Sure, no problem," Ben's mom replied. Ben's mom sat in the shade of a big maple tree watching the kids play.

"Steph and Ben get along just great," Darlene commented as she was walking back toward the table with the lemonade.

"They sure do," Ben's mom replied.

"So, Gloria told me she met Ben and Frank, but she did not get a chance to meet you yet."

"Yeah, my husband said she seemed like a nice lady, and that Ben and Jake got along just fine."

"Are you going to take Ben to Jake's birthday party on Saturday?" asked Darlene.

"Yes. Are you and Stephanie going to be there?" Ben's mom replied.

"You betcha. Stephanie and Jake have been playing for about a year now. Gloria moved out here after her husband died," Darlene told Ben's mom.

"Frank told me he had a heart attack. That is a horrible deal," Ben's mom said.

"Yes, she is a very strong women, and I think it is for Jake's sake that she remains strong," Darlene replied.

"I do not know what I would do if I were in her shoes," Ben's mom said as she was shaking her head back and forth.

"I don't think any of us would know unless it actually happened to us," Darlene said with a look of dismay. Their conversation was stopped there as Ben started to cry. He had fallen down on the concrete slab just outside the pool.

"Ben, are you alright?" his mom asked.

"I fall down!" Ben said as he was crying his eyes out.

"Oh sweetie, it is not that bad—it's just a little scrape. I think someone is ready for a nap," his mom said.

"Yeah, I want a Band-aide and go take a nap, Mommy," Ben replied.

"Tell Darlene and Stephanie thank you for letting you come over and swim," his mom told him.

"Tank you," he said as he was sniffling. He didn't even say thank you clearly.

"You're welcome, Ben, and we will see you at Jake's party Saturday," Darlene told him.

"Sounds good, and maybe he will swim longer next time," his mom replied as they headed for home.

JAKE'S PARTY

Ben was ready bright and early when Saturday morning came around. He couldn't wait for Jake's party to start; even though it was the break of dawn, he was ready to go.

"Wake up! Wake up!" Ben said as he was jumping up and down on his parents' bed. "Jake's party is today!" he said.

"I know, Ben, but it is not 'til one o'clock. It is only seven thirty in the morning," his dad said as he rolled back over and put a pillow over his head.

"I will get up with Ben, honey. You sleep a little longer," his mom told his dad.

"Thank you," his dad replied.

Ben and his mom were watching Saturday morning cartoons while they were eating their breakfast. "Ben, do you want to go pick Jake something out for his birthday?" his mom asked.

"Yeah, Mommy, Jake needs a plane," Ben said.

"Oh, he *does*, does he?" she replied.

"Yeah, and he needs someone to fly his plane," he added.

"Well, let's go wake Daddy up and see if he wants to go," she told him. She did not have to tell him twice. Ben took off running up the stairs, yelling the whole way.

"Daddy, Daddy, wake up! We are going to get Jake a plane!" he yelled.

"Oh, we are?" his dad replied with a tired grin on his face.

"Yeah, and we are going to find a man to fly his plane," Ben added.

"Ok, son. Let me get up and around," he told Ben as he was stretching, trying to wake his body up.

"O-tay, Dad. I'll go get my shoes on," Ben said.

"Ben, you will need your mom to get you some clothes," his dad said as he was laughing; Ben was still in his underwear.

They all got dressed and headed out their front door on a mission to find a plane and a guy to fly it. Ben and his parents went to three different stores before they found what they were looking for. Ben insisted on a plane for Jake and would not settle for anything else.

"Well, Ben, we finally found Jake a plane," his dad said with a look of relief.

"Yeah, and he's going to like this plane, Dad," Ben replied.

"I hope so. It took us long enough to find that plane!" his mom told him.

"Let's go get some lunch and then go to the party," his dad said.

When they pulled up in their driveway, Ben started yelling and throwing a fit. "I want to go to Jake's party!" Ben screamed at the top of his lungs.

"Ben, we are going to go through the house and then through the backyard to Jake's house," his mom said in a soothing voice.

"Ben, you have to get out of the car, or we will not go, and you can go in and take a nap," his dad told him.

They got Ben settled down; since he knew what the plan was, he was back in a good mood. As they were walking through their yard, they could hear children laughing and playing in Jake's yard. "Sounds like the party has started," Ben's dad said.

"It sure does. You hear that, Ben?" his mom asked.

"Yeah, Mom, I hear other kids back there!" he said.

"Let's get this party started, people!" Ben's dad yelled as he poked his head over Gloria's fence.

"Jake, Ben is here! Go open the gate for them," Gloria told him.

"Okay, Mom, I will" he said as he ran for the gate. Jake got to the gate, but was having a hard time trying to get it open. Ben's dad coached him through it, and after a minute or so, he got it. "Thanks for coming to my party," Jake said.

"Thanks for having us," Ben's mom replied.

"I got a plane for you, Jake," Ben said.

"Ben, it was supposed to be a *surprise*," his mom said.

"Oh, well. Go ahead and give it to him—the cat is out of the bag now!" his dad replied.

"Might as well. Here, Jake," she said as she handed him the red bag with the plane in it.

"Thank you, Ma'am," Jake said.

"Well, what a little gentleman. Did you hear that, Frank? He called me Ma'am," she said with a big smile on her face.

Ben took off with Jake to where all the other kids were. All the kids were huddled around the cement patio playing hopscotch. The parents were sitting around a green picnic table talking. Gloria was standing at the end of the table pouring punch into cups for the kids.

"Hey, Gloria, this is Ben's mom," Ben's dad told her.

"What is wrong?" asked Ben's mom. She could tell something was not right with Gloria.

"Oh, nothing much. D'you see the lady on the end?" Gloria asked.

"Yes," Ben's mom replied.

"Her name is Misty Burbank. She watches Jake and a few of the other kids I invited to the party," Gloria told her.

"Yeah, what about her?" Ben's mom asked.

"She is moving to Arizona, and I do not know who will watch Jake now while I am at work," Gloria replied.

"Well, I could watch him for you," Ben's mom told her.

"You would do that for me?" she asked.

"Yeah. I do not work—Frank makes enough for the both of us. Plus, that would give Ben someone else to play with during the day. Ben has Stephanie to play with, but she is not always there, and he gets bored easily."

"That would be great! He would be right next door, and I could head straight home after work." Gloria looked relieved at that moment and reached into her purse.

"Here is my card. It has my work phone number on it, so that if you have any problems or need anything during the day, you can call me," Gloria told her.

"Okay, so it is settled, then. We will see Jake Monday morning." Ben's mom said.

"Yes, and I will pay you fifty dollars Monday—that is, if fifty is enough for you?" Gloria remarked.

"Oh, you do not have to pay me anything. It would be doing *me* a favor, too," Ben's mom replied as she patted Gloria on the shoulder.

"No, I *want* to pay you something. It is non-negotiable," said Gloria in a firm voice.

"Okay, since you put it that way," Ben's mom replied. The situation that occurred led to Ben, Jake, and Stephanie becoming best friends. Stephanie's mom had to work three days out of the week, so Ben's mom watched her, too, and the three were inseparable. The next three years of their lives, they did just about everything together. They started school, t-ball, and even soccer together. The kids loved the fact that they could do all of these things together. Neither their parents nor the kids knew what the future would hold; only time would tell.

BEST FRIENDS

"Ben, get up. You need to eat breakfast, and your bus will be here in twenty minutes!" Ben's mom hollered up the stairs.

"I'm up, Mom. I'll be down in a minute," Ben replied.

It was October 10, 1993; Ben was seven years old. Every morning before school, Ben would meet Stephanie and Jake at the bus stop. After he finished his breakfast, he would head out the door.

"Bye, Mom!" Ben said.

"Bye, sweetie. I'll see you when you get home from school," his mom replied.

The door slammed before she could come around the corner and give him a hug. Ben was off for the bus stop. Ben's mom knew that his friends made him happy, and she was glad he had good friends.

"Hi, guys," Ben said as he was running up to the bus stop.

"Hi, Ben," Stephanie said.

"Where is your lunch, Ben?" asked Jake.

"Oh, man. I forgot it!" Ben said in an upset manner.

"You guys, hold the bus—I'm going to run home and get it." Ben darted around the corner of the shrubs that lined the sidewalk. To his surprise, his mom was coming down the sidewalk with his lunch pail.

"You missing something, honey?" his mom asked.

"Yeah, my lunch. I was running home to get it," Ben replied.

"You better hurry—you don't want to miss the bus, Ben."

"Thanks, Mom. 'Love you."

"I love you, too."

Every day after school, the three of them would rush home and get a snack, then meet in front of Ben's house on their bikes. Down the street from their homes was a small wooded area. Ben and Jake were riding their bikes past the wooded area one day when they noticed some old lumber laying in the trees. They decided to go see what was back there.

They walked into the trees and saw a clubhouse up in the highest tree in the bunch. This became their little place to go hang out, and for Ben, it was where he felt comfortable away from his house. Ben's dad was becoming more and more hateful toward his mom, and it made Ben uneasy when he acted like that. He would want to stay at the clubhouse rather than his own house. Jake and Stephanie had no idea about what was going on at Ben's house; they just thought he really loved the clubhouse and didn't want to leave.

This was Ben's first den, and when he was with Stephanie and Jake, he felt safe there. Other kids from the neighborhood would come by, and they would play different games in the wooded area around the clubhouse. Even though Ben wouldn't want to go home, he knew he couldn't stay there. Ben's mom would worry about him. Ben could not understand what his mom had done that would make his dad get so upset with her. No matter what the situation was, Ben felt bad for his mom and wanted to be there for her.

A few months later, Ben, Stephanie, and Jake were headed for their clubhouse after school one day. Just as they were arriving, Johnny, another kid from the neighborhood, was riding up, too.

"Hey, guys," Johnny said as he slid in with his bike.

"Hey, Johnny," they all said simultaneously.

"Hey, Jake, you want to go to my grandma's house with me tomorrow?" Johnny asked.

"Sure, did you already ask your parents if I could go?" Jake replied.

"Yeah, they said you could come. We just need to have your parents call mine so they can talk about it." Johnny told him.

"Well, I'll have to go ask my parents. You want to ride down to my house with me?" Jake asked.

"Sure. Let's go," said Johnny.

"I'll be back, guys," Jake told Ben and Stephanie.

Jake and Johnny peeled out with their bike tires and shot off down the road to Jake's house. Ben and Stephanie didn't really like Johnny too much. Johnny was the neighborhood bully, and was always trying to tell the other kids what to do.

"You want to go up to the clubhouse?" Ben asked Stephanie.

"Sure. I'll race you!" she replied.

They both took off, running for the tall oak where the clubhouse was. Ben came up to the bottom of the ladder first, and started up it. The ladder was one of those rope ones that hooked up to the deck of the clubhouse.

"Come back here! I'm going to win!" Stephanie told Ben.

"No, *I'm* going to win," said Ben.

Stephanie then reached up and grabbed Ben's shoe.

"Hey, give me my shoe back!" Ben yelled.

"Come get it, Ben," Stephanie said as she was shaking his shoe around, taunting him.

"Forget it—I don't need my shoe. I'm going to win," Ben told her as he made it to the top. When Ben made it to the top, he pulled himself in and went to the window on his right. That was the window facing Stephanie, who was still on the ground.

"Haha. I'm the winner, Steph!" Ben yelled.

"I don't care! I have your shoe, and you ain't getting it back." Stephanie replied.

All of a sudden, they could hear someone yelling.

"*Woohoo!*" It was Johnny.

Johnny and Jake were coming back from Jake's house. They were headed at full speed toward the clubhouse.

"Why does Stephanie have your shoe, Ben?" asked Jake.

"I grabbed it when he was going up the ladder," Stephanie told Jake.

"Ben, you got your shoe stolen by a girl. " Johnny yelled as he was laughing at Ben.

"Shut up, Johnny!" Ben yelled in frustration

"Why don't you make me?" Johnny replied.

Johnny was nine. Since he was a couple years older than the rest of them, he thought he could bully them around. Ben started coming down the ladder, and Johnny threw his bike down. When Ben got to the bottom, Stephanie gave Ben his shoe.

"I'm sorry, Ben—I was just playing around," she told him.

"It's alright," Ben replied.

Just when Ben leaned down to put his shoe on, Johnny ran up and pushed him on the ground.

"What are you doing? Leave him alone, Johnny!" Stephanie cried.

"You shut up, Stephanie. Don't you try and tell me what to do!" he told her as he pushed her down, too.

Ben got up and pushed Johnny back, but he was much bigger, so it didn't do much to him. Johnny then reared back and hit Ben in his chest. Ben went falling to the ground again and clinched his chest.

"Just *go*, Johnny!" Stephanie said as she was getting up.

"Yeah, Johnny—cut it out," Jake said with a pleading voice.

"You like these wimps? I thought you wanted to go with me to my grandma's house tomorrow," Johnny told him.

"I *do*," Jake replied.

"Then let's get out of here and leave these wimps behind!" Johnny said.

Jake looked down at Ben and Stephanie. He felt bad, but he didn't have the guts to stand up to Johnny. "Sorry, guys," Jake said as he got on his bike.

"You're going to leave with him?" Stephanie asked.

"Yeah, I'm going with him tomorrow," Jake replied as he started to ride off with Johnny.

"Fine, you go be his friend. I don't want to be your friend anymore!" Ben yelled at him.

Jake didn't even look back as he and Johnny rode off.

Stephanie then helped Ben get to his feet. "Let's go home, Ben," she said.

As Ben was riding home side-by-side with Stephanie, he started thinking about what he had said to Jake. Ben felt bad about what he had said, and he hoped that he and Jake would work it out in a few days. That was the first time Ben had ever talked to Jake that way.

Stephanie could see that Ben was upset over it. "Don't worry, Ben—I will always be your friend," Stephanie told him.

"I know, Steph. I will always be your friend, too," Ben replied. As Ben and Stephanie got to their houses, they said they would see each other in the morning.

Ben walked into his house, and his mom was cooking dinner. "Ben, is that you?" his mom asked.

"Yeah, Mom," he replied.

"Dinner is almost ready. Go wash up," she told him.

Ben went toward the bathroom and noticed that his dad was in the den, working. Ben poked his head around the corner; his dad didn't even notice him. "Hi, Dad," Ben said.

"Hi, son. How are you doing?" his dad asked.

"Okay," Ben replied. Ben noticed that his dad had one of his special drinks in front of him. The drink was nothing more than whiskey and coke, but all Ben knew was that his dad started getting more of an attitude with the more of those drinks he had. "Well, I've got to get washed up. I'll see you at dinner," Ben told his dad.

"Okay, son. I'll see you at the table," he replied.

After Ben washed up, he went into the dining room where his mom was setting the table. "Hi, Mom," Ben said.

"Hi, sweetie. Did you have fun with your friends?" she asked.

"Yeah, but—," Ben said as he sighed.

"What is wrong, Ben?" she asked.

"It's just…" He paused.

"Just *what*, Ben?" she said with an insisting voice.

"Johnny was there, too, and he was being a bully," He told her.

"You know I've told you to stay away from him," she said.

"I know, but he came down to our clubhouse and was calling me a wimp. I was going to fight him!" Ben said with a look of frustration.

"*Fight* him? You know you're not supposed to be fighting!" his mom told him.

"I know, Mom, but he pushed me and Steph down. Jake didn't even *do* anything—he left with him after that. I told Jake I didn't want to be his friend anymore," Ben told her as he was getting upset all over again.

"Well, I am sure you guys will be out playing again in a few days. You two will forget all about it and be friends again," she told him.

Just then, Ben's dad came into the dining room. Ben could tell dad had had too many of his special drinks. His dad walked in, sat down at the table, and started scooping piles of meatloaf onto his plate. All of a sudden, his dad went off.

"Damn it this meatloaf is dry," his dad yelled.

"I'm sorry, I—" his mom was cut off by his dad.

"You need to learn how to cook," he said as he threw a chunk of the meatloaf in her face.

Ben just sat there with his head down, hoping his dad would leave the room.

"I am going to get us some *real* food, Ben, so you don't have to eat this," his dad said as he was slurring his words. Ben's dad walked out of the dining room and into the kitchen. Ben could hear the sound of his dad's keys, and then the front door slammed. Ben's mom started to cry.

"Don't cry, Mom. I will eat it—I think this meatloaf is good," Ben told her, trying to comfort her.

That made his mom cry even harder as she got up and patted his head. Ben didn't understand why his dad was so mean to his mom. Ben's dad had never laid a hand on Ben, but the thought of it happening crossed Ben's mind from time to time.

"You just eat what you want, Ben, and I will run you a bath," his mom told him.

"Okay, Mom," Ben replied. Ben finished his food and then went upstairs where his mom had a bath ready for him. After he got out of the bath, he watched a movie with his mom. Ben's dad still had not come home, and it was getting late.

"You need to get up to bed, Ben," his mom told him.

"Alright, Mom," he replied.

"You get a good night's sleep, and tomorrow will be a brighter day, Ben," his mom said with a smile on her face.

"I love you, Mom," Ben told her.

"I love you, too, Ben. Good-night," she replied.

Ben went up to his room and got his pajamas on, then slid into bed. He lay there thinking about the day and hoping that Jake would not be mad at him for what he had said. The thought of them not being friends actually upset Ben. With all the thoughts going through his head and the long day coming to an end, he dozed off to sleep.

The next morning when Ben got up for school, he was in a better mood. Ben was ready to face the day and see what would happen with Jake and him.

"Ben, are you ready? It is Friday, your last day of school for the week," his mom yelled.

"Yeah, I'm ready," he replied. He walked down the stairs and headed for the front door.

His mom came around the corner with his lunch and a breakfast bar. "Here, sweetie—here's your lunch, and you can eat this on the way to the bus stop," she told him.

"Thanks, Mom," he said with a smile on his face.

"You're in a good mood this morning," his mom said.

"Yeah. I am ready for the school day and to see if Jake will be at the bus stop," he told his mom.

Ben's mom gave him a big hug, and Ben headed out the door. Ben knew his mom was always in a good mood, despite the fact that his dad was always treating her wrong. Ben wondered if his dad was ever in a good mood in the morning, because Ben never got to see his dad in the morning. Ben's dad was always gone by the time Ben woke up. Ben made it to the bus stop and was surprised that Jake was not there.

"Hi, Stephanie," Ben said.

"Hi, Ben," she replied.

"Where's Jake?" asked Ben.

"I don't know," Stephanie replied.

Justin, another kid that met at the bus stop, lived on the next block.

"I saw him riding his bike toward the school with Johnny," Justin told them.

"You did? Jake's mom doesn't let him ride his bike to school," Ben replied.

"Well, maybe his mom doesn't know," Justin told Ben.

Ben just looked toward the bus coming down the road. He thought to himself, *Maybe Jake and I won't be friends, after all.*

They all loaded onto the bus and went off to school. Jake ignored Ben the whole day at school; even at recess, where they would usually play soccer together. Ben acted like it didn't bother him, but it did. Jake would just look away when Ben would look his way.

Jake thought to himself, *I should go tell him I'm sorry*, but every time he got the urge to do it, Ben saw him coming and would run off to do something else. Ben was being stubborn, too, about the whole thing.

After Ben thought that Jake didn't want to be friends, he started acting the same way. When school was let out, Ben saw Jake riding off with Johnny toward the neighborhood.

"Ben, come on." He heard a voice hollering at him. He turned around; it was Stephanie standing at the bus waiting for him. Ben smiled and went toward the bus. He was really glad he still had Stephanie as a friend. She was the first friend he had made when he moved into the neighborhood, and he was certain they would always be friends. Ben knew there was something about her that stood out from the rest of the kids. At the age of seven, though, he just couldn't figure out what it was.

TRAGEDY

It was Saturday morning, and Ben's mom was in the kitchen cooking breakfast. Ben was still in bed, and his dad was at the office as usual. The phone in the kitchen started to ring. Every time the phone rang, Ben's mom had a habit of looking at the time. It was 8:06 a.m. when she picked up the phone.

"Hello. Cassel residence," she said. "Calm down— what is wrong?" she asked. There was a long pause from his mom, and then she dropped the phone. "Ben, wake up, honey." Ben's mom was fighting back tears.

"What is wrong, Mom? Is Daddy being mean, again?" he asked.

"No, honey. I need you to sit up," she told him.

At this point, Ben knew there was something very wrong; he could see it in her face.

"Sweetie, Jake was in an accident," she said, trying not to cry.

"An accident? Is he alright?" Ben asked.

"He was at Johnny's grandma's house, and she lives on a busy street…" she paused.

"What, Mom—*what?*" Ben said with a concerned voice.

"Well, Jake ran into the street after a ball. He did not pay attention and ran out in front of a car. The car tried to stop—it just didn't have enough time," she told him.

"Is he going to be alright, Mom?" Ben asked as his eyes were filling up with tears.

"They rushed him to the hospital right away, and they tried all night to keep him alive. He passed away early this morning, sweetie. I'm so sorry," she replied.

Ben jumped out of bed and ran to the bathroom.

His mom went to the door of the bathroom; she was unsure of what she should do. "Ben, come out and talk to me, honey," she told him.

"No, Mom!" he said as he was bawling his eyes out.

"I know this hurts, sweetie, but we should talk about it," she told him.

Ben slowly opened the door, knowing that if anyone could help him through this, it would be his mom. "Mom, I told him I didn't want to be his friend anymore. I didn't get the chance to say I was sorry." Ben then embraced his mom.

"You know, I'm sure Jake was sorry for what happened, too. You guys were too close not to be sorry for what happened. You need to remember all the good things you guys did and not that one bad moment," she told him.

"You really think he was sorry, Mom?" asked Ben.

"I know he was, sweetie," she replied.

The days were long and slow leading up to Jake's funeral. At the kids' school, they were mourning the death of Jake, also. Jake was a loved kid in the community, and would be missed dearly. The day of his funeral, they called school off so that anyone who wanted to attend could do so. Ben and his parents were at home getting ready when their doorbell rang.

"I'll get it," Ben's dad said. "Ben, it's for you!" he yelled.

Ben went walking toward the front door. As he got closer, he couldn't believe whom it was.

"Hi, Ben. I am sorry about Jake. I know you guys were best friends. I also wanted to apologize for what happened at the clubhouse that day—I hope you can forgive me," Johnny said.

Ben couldn't believe Johnny was at his front door, but for some reason, his apology eased Ben's mind. "It's alright, Johnny. I know Jake was sorry, too. Thanks for the apology," Ben told him.

"Well, if you want to play sometime, come on over. That is, if it is okay with your parents," Johnny replied.

"Okay, Johnny. I'll see you later," Ben said. Ben closed the door and walked toward his living room. Something seemed different about Johnny; he seemed nicer, or maybe he was just being nice because of what had happened to Jake. Either way, Ben knew he would not be going to Johnny's house any time soon. Even though he'd apologized, Ben was still bitter over what had happened at the clubhouse.

After the funeral was over, there was a memorial dinner for Jake.

"You want to go to the dinner, Ben?" his mom asked.

"No, I just want to go home, Mom," Ben replied. He was still teary eyed.

"Alright, sweetie. Frank, come over here," his mom hollered.

"What, honey?" his dad asked.

"Ben just wants to go home," she said.

"Come on, Ben, let's go home," his dad said as he gave Ben a big hug.

Ben thought to himself, *My dad doesn't hug me very often. Maybe we should stay if my dad is going to be nice to Mom and me.* The thought didn't last very long, as the memories of Jake overwhelmed him again.

Several months passed, and Ben just wasn't his normal self. Stephanie had asked Ben out several times to play, and Ben just wasn't up to it. Ben's great uncle Kirk was the one that got Ben to snap out of his depressed mood.

"Kirk is here, Ben!" his mom yelled.

Ben was silent, and his mom waited for a reply.

"I'll go up to his room and talk to him," Kirk said.

"Alright. Maybe you can get him to come back to life—he has been dead to the world the past few months," his mom said.

Kirk went up to Ben's room and slowly opened his door.

"Ben, what are you doing, buddy?" Kirk asked.

Ben was sitting in his beanbag chair in front of his TV, watching cartoons. "Why does God take people from us, Uncle Kirk?" Ben asked.

"Well, Ben, sometimes we don't understand God's intentions. You can always count on his intentions being what is best for the circle of life," Kirk told him.

"The circle of life?" Ben said with a confused look on his face.

"Ben, people are born, and people die; in between those two, we live. The choices we make in our lives can dictate how long we get to live it. Jake made a mistake, Ben. When he went for that ball, he didn't look to see if there were any cars coming first. Unfortunately, that mistake cost him his life. You should always think before you act, Ben; that way, you've got a better shot at not making a big mistake," Kirk told him.

Ben got up from his beanbag chair. He then walked over and gave Kirk a big hug.

"Thanks, Uncle Kirk. I think I understand a little better now," Ben told him.

"Just remember, Jake loved Jesus and learning about him, so he is in a better place now," Kirk replied. They sat and talked for about thirty more minutes. When they were done, Kirk knew what would finish cheering Ben up. "Come on Ben, I'll take you out for ice cream," Kirk said.

"Can Mom come?" Ben asked. He was so excited; he loved ice cream.

"Sure, you know your Mom is welcome to go, too," Kirk replied.

Ben took off running out of his bedroom.

"Mom! Mom!" Ben cried.

"What, sweetie?" his mom said with a concerned voice.

"Uncle Kirk is going to take us out for ice cream," Ben told her.

She thought to herself *Is that all? He didn't have to come out hollering—I thought something was wrong.* She was glad she only thought it and didn't say it. Ben's mom was happy that she had her Ben back, and didn't want that to ever change again.

"Well, let's get going, then," she said as she winked at Kirk.

Ben shot out the front door, running for the car. Ben's mom stopped Kirk before they went out the door.

"What did you say to him?" she asked.

"Let's just say he understands a little bit more about life. This is a big step in his life, and I think he is going to be just fine. Now, let's go get some ice cream," Kirk said as he smiled.

After they got back from eating ice cream, Ben decided to go next door and see if Stephanie wanted to play.

"Mom, can I go see if Stephanie wants to play?" he asked.

"Sure, sweetie—you need to get out of this house. You go right ahead," she replied.

"Yeah, I'm ready now," he said. As Ben was heading for the front door, his mom stopped him.

"Ben, I'm proud of you, sweetie," she told him.

"Thanks, Mom," he replied.

That just lifted his spirit even more as he went out the door to play.

Ben and Stephanie became like one; they were always together. What Ben and Stephanie didn't expect, though, was for Johnny to ever be one of their friends.

Ben and Stephanie would ride down to Ben's Uncle Kirk's house and visit him almost every day. Johnny's house was right around the corner from Kirk's house. One day, Ben and Stephanie were headed to Kirk's when they heard a voice yelling at them. They couldn't see who it was.

"Who is that?" asked Ben.

"Come out so we can see you!" Stephanie hollered.

"It's me," Johnny said as he crawled out of some hedges by the road.

"Hey, Johnny," Ben said.

"Where're you guys going?" asked Johnny.

"We are going to my Uncle Kirk's house," Ben said.

"Can I hang out with you guys?" asked Johnny.

"I don't think so, Johnny," Stephanie replied as she was waving her hand.

"I'm not mean like I used to be, guys. I'm tired of not having any friends. I changed so that people would hang out with me," Johnny told them.

"Alright, Johnny—we'll give you a chance. If you're mean to Stephanie or me even one time, though, then we will never be your friend again," Ben told him.

"Alright, it's a deal. I promise I won't be mean," Johnny replied.

For some reason, Ben believed Johnny, but he knew only time would tell if he was truly sincere. They rode up to Uncle Kirk's house, and he was out on the porch, as usual.

"Hey, Uncle Kirk," Ben said.

"Hey, kids. What are you guys out stirring up?" he asked.

"Nothing, Uncle—we just came over to see you," Ben replied.

The reality of it for Ben was that he could get away from his house by going to visit his uncle. Ben's dad was sick that day and didn't go to work. Ben didn't want to be there in case his dad decided to start drinking. When his dad started drinking, he was also mean to his mom. Ben felt guilty sometimes for leaving his mom when his dad was home. Any time Ben would say something, though, his mom would tell him not to worry about it. Ben's mom would tell him that "she was a big girl," and "she would be all right."

Ben knew his mom was right about a lot of things, but he wasn't so sure when it came to this subject. Even though Ben was out playing with Stephanie, nine times out of ten they would end up at his uncle's house. Ben's den had changed from an old ragged clubhouse to his Uncle Kirk's house. The comfort of being at Kirk's house would ease Ben's mind. Kirk would always have something to tell him about life, and he would always put it in terms Ben could understand. There were times that Stephanie would have to go home, and Ben would stay at Kirk's house. Ben knew that Kirk would always be there for him.

THE PERFECT GIFT

A few years had passed, and Ben, Stephanie, and Johnny were all good friends. Stephanie had become a tomboy. There weren't any other girls her age in the neighborhood, so she just did what the boys would do. From sports to spitting, she would do it all.

The date was March 12, 1996. Ben was almost ten years old, and was starting to sprout up pretty well. Stephanie's tenth birthday was in eight days, and Ben wanted to get her a great gift.

"Mom, Stephanie's birthday is next Wednesday, and I don't know what to get her," he told his mom.

"Well, Ben, you and Stephanie have been friends a long time. You need to get her something very special," she replied.

"Like what, Mom?" Ben asked.

"I'll get my purse, Ben, and we will go to the store," his mom told him.

Ben and his mom loaded up in the car and went to the local department store. When they got to the store, Ben couldn't decide where to start.

"We can go anywhere you want, Ben," his mom said.

"Let's go to the games, Mom," Ben told her.

They paced up and down the aisles, but nothing really caught Ben's eye. He saw a couple of board games that she might like, but decided against them. They weren't what he was looking for. He wanted something that would express to Stephanie that he was glad to have such a good friend. As they were coming out of the game section, Ben noticed a sign hanging down from the ceiling. On it was a heart split in two, and on each necklace, it said "Best Friends Forever."

That is it, Ben thought to himself. The necklace was what he was getting for her.

"Mom, I want to get *that*," he said as he pointed at the sign.

"Ben, that is perfect," his mom replied.

They purchased the necklace and then got some lunch. When they got back to the car, Ben's mom was very impressed with Ben's choice.

"Ben, you have a good heart. Don't ever forget that. This world is full of too much hate and ugliness, Ben. The world needs more of you Bens in it," she told him as she started to tear up.

"Well, I got it from you, Mom," Ben replied.

Ben's mom started to cry even harder.

"What's wrong, Mom," Ben asked.

"Nothing, sweetie—I'm just so proud of you, and I would do anything for you. You know that, right?" she told him.

"Yes, Mom. Please don't cry," he asked.

"These are tears of joy, Ben, tears of joy," she replied.

Stephanie's party came a lot quicker than Ben was expecting. He knew it was a week ago that he had bought the necklace, but it seemed like yesterday. Stephanie had invited a few of her friends from school, and her cousins were there, too.

When the time came for presents, Ben was hanging around the back of the living room. Everyone was huddled around Stephanie as she sat on her sofa waiting to open her presents. Stephanie started to open her presents; one by one she was getting closer to the end. Ben was clenching the little box with a bow that had the necklaces in it. He was worried that the other kids were going to make fun of him.

"Ben, why are you standing back there?" asked Darlene.

"Oh, I'm just waiting my turn to give Steph her present," he replied.

"Oh, Ben, just go give it to her. You guys are best friends," her mom told him as she patted his back.

She's right—we have been best friends for what seems like forever. I don't care what anyone thinks, Ben told himself. Ben then walked right through the crowd of kids and went straight up to Stephanie.

"Here, Steph," Ben said as he handed her her present.

"Why thank you, Ben. I was wondering where you were," Stephanie told him.

Stephanie then started to open her present. As she raised the lid and looked inside, her eyes lit up.

"Ben, this is the best gift I've ever gotten!" she said with excitement. She then jumped up and gave Ben a hug.

Edward Terrell Sr.

"I just wanted you to know that you are my best friend," Ben told her.

"I know—and you are mine," she replied. She then put his necklace around his neck, and he put hers around her neck. Darlene looked at the two and thought to herself, *What a fairytale that would be—the two of them growing up and spending the rest of their lives together.* She then just smiled.

Ben woke up the next morning and ate breakfast at an unusually fast pace. He then headed out the door to his Uncle Kirk's house. Stephanie was at her grandma's house, so Ben was going to his uncle's house by himself that day. Ben rode up to Kirk's driveway and noticed that Kirk was not sitting on his porch. Ben thought that was weird because Kirk would usually be on his front porch drinking coffee in the morning.

"Uncle Kirk, where are you at?" asked Ben.

Ben got no reply, so he started banging on his door. After a couple of minutes, Kirk came strolling to the door and opened it.

"Ben, what are you doing here this morning? You don't have school today?" Kirk asked.

"No, Uncle, we are on spring break," Ben replied.

"Oh, spring break, huh?" he said. His uncle started coughing a lot more than usual, and couldn't stop. After a minute or so, his coughing settled down.

"Come on in, Ben," he told him.

They went to the kitchen, and Ben sat down at the table. "You want some breakfast, Ben?" Kirk asked.

"No, thanks. I already ate breakfast, but some orange juice sounds good," Ben replied.

"Go ahead and help yourself. You know where everything is," Kirk told him. Kirk made himself some eggs and bacon, and then he brewed a fresh pot of coffee. They sat there quietly while Kirk ate his breakfast. When he was finished, Ben grabbed his plate from him and took it to the sink.

"Thanks, Ben. You're a good boy," Kirk told him as he sipped his coffee. He then told Ben to sit down. "Ben, I need to talk to you—man to man," Kirk said as he was rubbing his head.

"What is it, Uncle?" Ben replied.

"Well, Ben, you like apple pie?" his uncle asked.

"Yeah, you got some?" Ben asked.

"No. Maybe we'll get some later," Kirk said as he sighed. "Ben, life is like apple pie. It is made with good apples and bad apples," he said.

Ben just kind of nodded; he wasn't quite sure what Kirk was getting at.

"Ben, I've been served a bad piece of pie, and I can't return it," Kirk said.

"A bad piece? Did it make you sick?" Ben asked.

"Yeah, you can say that," Kirk replied as he grabbed Ben's shoulder.

"You got a lot of good pieces of pie coming your way, Ben. Make sure you make the best of them," Kirk told him.

"Alright, Uncle Kirk," Ben replied. Ben was still a little confused, but knew it would make sense one day. "You want to go to the fishing hole, Uncle?" asked Ben.

"No, Ben, I'm not up to it today. Why don't you go see if Johnny will go with you?" he told him.

"Okay, Uncle. I'll see you later," Ben said. Ben left and went down to Johnny's to see if he was home. Ben got up to the door and realized there were no cars there. He rang the doorbell and waited, but nobody came to the door. Ben then jumped on his bike and headed home. When he got home, his dad was pulling into the driveway.

"Yeah, Ben, I've come home early today. Do you want to go fishing or something?" his dad asked.

"Sure, Dad—that's what I was wanting to do, but I couldn't find anyone to go with me," Ben told him.

"Well, let's get our poles loaded up, and we'll go to the lake for the day," his dad said.

The two of them got the truck loaded with their fishing gear and headed to the lake. When they got out there, they found a good shaded area on the bank. They got all their gear situated and put their lines in the water.

"You ready to catch a big catfish?" Ben's dad asked.

"I'm going to catch the biggest one in the lake, Dad," Ben replied.

Ben and his dad spent the afternoon fishing, and Ben really enjoyed the time they spent together. Ben knew his dad was a busy man, trying to keep the business running smoothly. Ben just wished his dad had more time to spend with him. The other kids in the neighborhood were always going and doing things with their dads, and it would make Ben a little jealous. Ben would just tell himself that his dad was a busy man, and he needed to be at his office so the employees knew what to do. Ben was always making excuses for his dad; it was his way of easing his mind. What Ben didn't know, though, was that one day the real reasons would be revealed.

LIFE'S NOT FAIR

The next morning, Ben woke up in a very good mood. He ran down the stairs, hoping that his dad was home.

"Mom, is Dad home?" he said with an excited voice.

"No, sweetie, he's at work," she replied.

Ben lowered his head and walked into the living room. He sat down on the couch next to his mom.

"What is wrong, Ben?" his mom asked.

"I had a lot of fun with Dad yesterday, and I was hoping he was home again today," Ben told his mom.

"You know your dad's work is very important to him," she told him.

Ben just wished that *he* were more important than his dad's work. Instead of talking more about it, Ben just asked for some breakfast. After Ben ate breakfast, he went down to Johnny's to see if he wanted to play. As he was almost to Johnny's, he saw Johnny riding his bike down the road.

"Hey, Johnny, what are you doing?" Ben yelled.

"I'm going down to Justin's to play soccer. You want to go?" Johnny asked.

"Sure. 'Sounds like fun," Ben replied.

They both raced for Justin's house. They spent a couple of hours playing soccer at Justin's. When they were done, Ben asked Johnny if he wanted to go to his Uncle Kirk's house with him.

"Sure, but I can't stay long. I have to go home and check-in with my mom in an hour," Johnny told him.

As Ben and Johnny were rounding the corner, Ben noticed that his Dad's truck was at his uncle's house. Ben and Johnny left their bikes on the curb in the front yard. As they were walking up to the house, Ben's dad was coming out the front door.

"Where is Uncle Kirk, Dad?" Ben asked.

"Ben, sit down on the porch. I need to talk to you," his dad told him.

Ben saw it in his dad's face; it was the same kind of look his mom had the morning she came in to tell him about Jake. Ben started to tear up and ran to his bike.

"Ben, stop—Ben, just talk to me, son!" his dad yelled.

There was nothing anyone could have said to stop him. Ben rode so fast that even Johnny couldn't catch up with him. Ben's dad went back in the house and called Ben's mom. When she answered the phone, Ben's dad was really upset on the other end of the line.

"Ben showed up here at Kirk's while I was getting some papers. He knew something was wrong, and I tried to talk to him, but he took off on his bike," he was explaining to her.

Before his dad could say anymore, his mom cut him off.

"I'm pretty sure I know where he is. I'll go talk to him," she told him.

"Okay. I've got to go back to the hospital to take care of some things. I will be home later," his dad told her.

Ben had gone down to the old clubhouse to try and get away from everybody. He wasn't even there ten minutes when he heard the sound of car tires on the gravel. Ben looked out the window that faced the road, and through the trees he could see his mom coming toward the clubhouse.

"Ben, are you up there? Ben, if you're up there, you need to answer me…" she yelled.

Ben slowly poked his head out the window. "What do you want?" Ben asked with a snotty attitude.

"I want to talk to you. Can I come up?" she replied.

"If you can make it," Ben told her.

Ben's mom climbed the ladder, and when she got to the top, she crawled in the clubhouse. Ben was sitting in the corner curled up in a ball.

"Ben, Uncle Kirk has been really sick the past three months. Six months ago, doctors found cancer in his body. The cancer had already spread too far for them to do anything about it," she told him.

Right then, Ben knew what Kirk had meant when he told him he'd was served a bad piece of apple pie.

"Why didn't you guys tell me about it?" he asked.

"Sweetie, you were so close to Uncle Kirk. We didn't want you to spend the last days of his life wondering whether he would be there every day," she told him. Ben's mom embraced him and started rubbing his head. She knew Ben was upset and wanted to find the right thing to say.

"Ben, you remember when Jake passed away and you were so upset because you didn't get the chance to tell him how you felt?" she asked.

"Yes, Mom," he replied.

"Well, you should be happy that you had a really good relationship with uncle Kirk all the way up to the end. Everyone passes away, sweetie, and those of us that are still around should be thankful we had the chance to be at peace with those who pass," she told him.

"I guess you're right, Mom, but I still will miss him," Ben said as he shrugged his shoulders.

"I know, sweetie, but just remember he will always be in our hearts," she replied.

They sat there, as his mom held him and let him cry it out. When he was finished, she told him she was making spaghetti and meatballs for dinner. Ben smiled because this was one of his favorite meals.

"I am pretty hungry, Mom," he said.

"Well, let's go home. We can go get a couple good movies and spend the rest of the day together," she replied.

"That sounds good," Ben said with a happier attitude.

The passing of Ben's Uncle Kirk wasn't as hard on Ben as the passing of Jake. Ben was a little older when Kirk passed, and it helped that Ben was on good terms with him when it happened. Ben started to confide more in Stephanie as they got older. Ben and Stephanie were twelve years old, and the neighborhood was pretty much the same as it had been when they first met. There was one addition, though; Jackie Conner and her family moved in three houses down from Stephanie.

Ben and Stephanie slowly became friends with her. Jackie was a lot different than all the other kids in the neighborhood. She was not very polite, and she liked causing mischief. The first three months she was there, she was grounded four times. The last time she was grounded was for starting a fire in the field down the street. The town police decided to let her parents handle her and warned her that the next time, she wouldn't be so lucky. She was lucky; they put out the fire quickly and it did not burn anything but grass.

Ben and Stephanie were on their way to Johnny's house one day when they ran into Jackie. Jackie was sitting on the corner with her head down, picking blades of grass. Jackie heard them coming down the road and raised her head.

"Hey, guys," Jackie said.

Ben and Stephanie acted like they didn't hear her at first.

"Hey guys, can I hang out with you?" Jackie asked with a pleading voice.

Stephanie slowed down, then stopped, and Ben stopped behind her.

"What are you doing, Steph?" asked Ben.

"If we let you hang out with us, you can't be starting any fires. We don't like getting in trouble either, so don't you think about doing something stupid," Stephanie told her.

"Oh, I won't. I promise. Let me go grab my bike," Jackie replied.

From that day forward, there was a group of four that were always together: Ben, Stephanie, Johnny, and now Jackie. Life was going well for Ben at this time in his life. He really liked Stephanie, but didn't know how to tell her. Ben just didn't want to make her mad in the case that she didn't feel the same way. Ben was scared she wouldn't even be his friend then. Instead of chancing it, he just kept it to himself.

The four of them went through middle school having a blast. Ben and Johnny made the football, basketball, and baseball teams. They were quite the athletes, and everyone in the town knew it. Stephanie and Jackie were the top cheerleaders at the school. Every sport they had cheer-leaders for had Stephanie and Jackie cheering them on. Ben was so happy with the way his life was going that he couldn't wait for high school to start. Eighth grade sum-mer had come, and all that the four of them talked about was starting their freshman year.

STEPHANIE
IS GONE

Ben woke up at about 10:00 a.m. on June 6, 2000. He went to the kitchen to eat breakfast and noticed that his mom wasn't anywhere around. Ben then looked out the back patio door and saw his mom in her garden. Ben noticed his mom was doing a lot more gardening the past few years. He wasn't sure why, but she seemed at peace when she was in her garden. He ate his breakfast and then headed out to talk to his mom.

"Mom, are you having fun?" Ben asked.

"Of course, Ben. Can't you tell?" she replied.

"No," Ben told her as he smiled. "You need a drink, Mom? You look hot," Ben asked.

"Sure, sweetie, I'll take iced tea if you don't mind," she told him.

"Sure, Mom. Anything for you," he replied as he went toward the house to fix her some iced tea. Just when he was pouring the last bit of tea, the doorbell rang. Ben just knew it was one of his friends, so he ran for the front door and swung it open.

"What's up?" Ben said.

On the other side of the threshold was Stephanie, and she was very upset. Stephanie had been crying—Ben could tell—and she was trying to hide it. When she looked into Ben's eyes, she started flowing like Niagara Falls.

"What is wrong?" asked Ben.

"My…My…" She couldn't spit it out.

"Slow down. Calm down, Steph," Ben told her. Ben then sat down with her on the front porch so he could get her to calm down. After a few minutes, she relaxed and was ready to talk.

"My dad got a new job, and…" She started to cry again. "We have to move to another state, Ben," she told him.

Ben just sat there and didn't know what to say. Just when life seemed to be going well, it served Ben a bad piece of apple pie.

"Well, when are you guys moving?" Ben asked.

"We have to leave next month," she replied.

"Well, we will have to write a lot of letters to keep up with each other," Ben told her.

Stephanie smiled; she couldn't believe how positive Ben was about it. She could tell he was upset, but somehow, he always had something good to say.

"I wanted to tell you first—that way you wouldn't hear it from someone else," she told him.

"It will all work out, Steph. I will come by later, and we'll go do something to cheer you up," Ben said.

"Alright. I'll see you later," Stephanie replied.

Ben watched Stephanie as she walked back toward her house. What she had told him was actually sinking in. Ben went back inside to go get his mom's tea and take it to her. He walked back to the garden area and handed his mom her tea. Ben had a sad and worried look on his face.

"What's wrong, Ben?" his mom asked. She could tell there was something not right.

"Steph just stopped by…" Ben paused.

"…And?" she said.

"Her dad got a new job, and they have to move next month," Ben said with disappointment.

"Well, that's life, Ben. The only thing you can be sure of is that everything changes eventually," his mom told him.

"I suppose you're right," Ben replied.

"Just make sure you go spend as much time as possible with her. Who knows—maybe we'll go visit her one day," she told him.

Ben was glad his mom was always so positive. Even though things seemed to be falling apart, she would always find something positive to say.

"Thanks, Mom. I'm going to go to Stephanie's right now," he said with a smile.

"You go enjoy yourself and make the best of this summer break," his mom replied.

Ben spent as much time every day as he could with Stephanie. When the morning came for Stephanie and her family to leave, Ben and his parents went over to see them off.

"Well, you guys take care of yourselves," Ben's dad told Jack.

"We will. You guys do the same," Jack replied.

Ben's mom and Stephanie's mom embraced, and they started to cry. They were pretty close, too, and they knew the chances of seeing each other again were slim. Stephanie was in the back yard getting her bike, and Ben went back there to say good-bye.

"I'll write you once a week," Ben said.

"And I will be looking forward to your letters so that I can write you back," she replied.

"Just keep that necklace on that I bought you, and I will keep mine on, too. We will always have each other this way," Ben told her.

Ben then gave her a big hug and a peck on the cheek. He stood back, hoping it didn't make her feel uncomfortable. Stephanie looked at him in the eyes, and then she laid a big wet one on his lips.

"I'll never forget you, Ben," she said as she was fighting back tears.

Stephanie took off toward the front yard, and Ben followed behind her. He couldn't help but think to himself that he should have told her how he felt. It was too late now; she was getting in the car, and he didn't want to be embarrassed in front of the adults. Instead, he bit his tongue and watched his best friend and the girl he loved drive down the road. Ben then hoped it would not be the last time he saw Stephanie.

The summer flew by, and the three left in the bunch were ready for high school to start. The first day of school just wasn't the same without Stephanie. Even though he wrote Stephanie once a week, and they would talk on the phone every other day, he still missed her. They used to always talk about their first day of high school, and it was still hard to believe she wasn't there. Ben was happy she was still alive, though. The other people in his life that had left him had passed on. He knew at least that there was a chance he could see Stephanie again.

As Ben's freshman year was rolling forward, Ben started making other friends. Ben, Johnny, and Jackie started hanging out on the other side of town. A kid named Cameron Pots lived on that side of town. Cameron was well known for the shenanigans he would pull. The kids on that side of town would always give Ben, Johnny, and Jackie crap because they lived on the nice side of town. The side of town that Cameron lived on didn't have wealthy families in it, and the houses were not in great shape.

Ben and Johnny would meet up with the other kids at the *Hall* after football practice. The Hall was a rundown pool hall that had arcade games in it, too. The kids from the high school would meet there and then spread out to other parts of town. Ben and Cameron were the best at air hockey and would always challenge each other to a game. One day after they'd finished a game, Cameron asked Ben to come with him.

"Hey, Ben, you and Johnny want to see something cool?" Cameron asked.

"I guess. What is it?" Ben replied.

"You do or you don't. You'll see what it is when you get there," Cameron told him.

"Sure—let me go get Johnny," Ben said.

Ben walked over to tell Johnny. Johnny was shooting a game of pool with Trey Walker. Trey was the kicker on the football team.

"Johnny, let's go—Cameron has something cool to show us," Ben told him.

"What is it?" Johnny asked.

"I don't know. We'll see when we get there," Ben replied.

"Alright, let's go. I'll see you later, Trey," Johnny said.

The three of them were getting ready to take off when Jackie was coming down the sidewalk with a couple other girls.

"Where're you guys going, Ben?" Jackie asked.

"It's none of your business, Jackie," Cameron said.

"Shut up, Cameron. I wasn't talking to you," Jackie replied.

"We're going somewhere with Cameron," Ben told her.

"Can I go?" she asked.

"No, it's a secret, and I'm only showing Ben and Johnny," Cameron said.

"Fine, then—I'll just go in the Hall and hang out," Jackie said as she gave Cameron the middle finger.

Ben kind of felt bad for Jackie, but he didn't want to catch crap from Cameron, so he didn't say anything. The three of them took off down the sidewalk headed to wherever it was Cameron was taking them. Right on the outside of town was a big bridge that passed over a ditch. There was a bike path that would lead them down under the bridge. Cameron was going really quickly down the hill when all of a sudden he veered off the path and into some tall grass.

"Where are you going, Cameron?" Johnny yelled.

"There is a jump over here, and it leads to a path we made. Come on!" Cameron replied.

Ben and Johnny followed, making sure they were very cautious not to hit any big holes. When they made it down to the bottom of the ditch, there was a big area that looked like a fort made of rocks. The rocks were stacked on top of each other, making three different walls.

"This is pretty cool," Ben said.

"This is where a few other people and I come to hang out. You two seem cool, so I thought I would invite you out this Friday to party with us," Cameron told them.

"Party? That sounds fun," Johnny said with intrigue.

"This Friday, Trey, Mark, and I are going to invite some girls down here, and Mark's big brother is going to get us some beer. You guys want to join in on the fun?" Cameron asked.

"Sure," Johnny wasted no time with his answer.

Ben kind of hesitated, and after a long pause, he answered Cameron.

"Yeah. I'm in, too," Ben said.

"Cool. We'll all meet at the Hall after the game Friday. Mark's brother will meet us there, too. After we give him some money for the beer, we'll come down here to party," Cameron told them.

The three of them rode back to the Hall, and about thirty minutes later, Ben was ready to go home.

"Hey, Johnny, Jackie—I'm headed home, you guys want to come?" Ben asked.

"I'm going to Trey's house," Johnny said.

"I'll go with you," Jackie replied.

Ben and Jackie told their friends good-bye and headed for home. On the way home, Ben told Jackie about the party Friday night. Ben took his time telling her about it. He wanted her to go with him, but was beating around the bush.

"So, are you inviting me to go, Ben?" Jackie asked.

"Yeah, I guess I am," he replied.

"Have you ever drunk beer before?" she asked.

"No, but there's a first time for everything," Ben replied.

"Yeah. I'll be there," she said, laughing about what he said.

THE BIG GAME

When Friday came around, the day was flying by for Ben. He was excited about the little party they were planning. As Ben and Johnny were suiting up for the game, the party was all they could talk about.

"I invited Jessica Welch," Johnny told Ben.

"That's cool. She seems like a cool chick. I asked Jackie to go," Ben told him.

"You asked *Jackie*?" Johnny said with surprise.

"Yeah—what's the big deal?" Ben said.

"You know, we're all going to be trying to round bases tonight," Johnny told him.

"Yeah, I know. Do you think I'm stupid, Johnny?" Ben said.

"You think *Jackie* is gong to let you on her field?" Johnny asked.

"I don't know. It might be worth a shot, though. She's pretty hot, and I've liked her for a while now," Ben told Johnny.

"Hey, she's hot, but she's also Jackie. She is a tough girl, Ben," Johnny replied.

"Yeah, well, I'm not scared," Ben said.

They both slammed their lockers closed and headed for the field.

Ben played running back, and Johnny was the right guard. Ben loved running the ball behind Johnny; he was a big boy. Johnny was already six foot two, 225 pounds his freshman year. Ben was five foot eight, 165, and he was fast. Ben had broken off tackles all night and scored three touchdowns. They ended up winning the game twenty-eight to seventeen, and the town was excited. That was the first time in five years that their school had beaten their rivals.

After the game, Ben's mom was in the parking lot waiting on him.

"Ben, you played an awesome game, honey, I'm so proud of you!" his mom said as she hugged him to death.

"Alright, Mom, you're going to crack my ribs. Thanks for coming tonight. Where is Dad?" Ben asked, but he already knew the answer.

"He's at the office, I guess," she replied.

Ben really wished his dad could have been there that night. Nevertheless, he was used to it by now. His mom could see the disappointment in his eyes and gave him another hug. For some reason, Ben never got embarrassed when his mom would hug him in front of people. He would see other kids shy away from their parents. Ben loved his mom too much, and nothing she did bugged him. She was always there for him—rain or shine.

"Hey, Mom, some friends are going to hang out at the Hall for awhile tonight. Is it alright if I go?" Ben asked.

"Sure, sweetie. You want a ride?" she asked.

"No, me and Johnny are riding our bikes over there," He replied.

"Well, here—take this and make sure you get you something to eat, Ben," she told him as she handed him twenty dollars.

"Alright, Mom, I will," he said.

"*Come on,* Ben!" Johnny yelled from across the parking lot.

"I got to go, Mom—I'll see you at home," Ben told her.

"Be home at eleven!" she yelled as he was riding off through the parking lot.

"Alright, Mom!" he yelled back.

When Ben and Johnny showed up at the Hall, there were already people there. They walked in, and everyone was chanting Ben's name. Ben couldn't help but smile, and it was no little smile.

"Hey, I threw him a lot of blocks. How do you think he got all those touchdowns?" Johnny told everyone.

"I saw the block you missed and then fell on your ass!" Cameron said as everyone started laughing.

"How 'bout I throw you on *your* ass," Johnny told Cameron as he started to walk toward him.

"Calm down, big boy. I was just joking," Cameron said.

"So am I. I won't kick your ass. Besides, I'm tired from the game anyway," Johnny said.

"Hey, you and Ben meet me over at the farthest pool table in a minute," Cameron told Johnny quietly.

Johnny went over and got Ben, then walked over to the pool table.

"Either one of you guys got money to pitch in on some beer?" Cameron asked.

"I got some," Ben replied.

"Mark's brother is going to be here in a few minutes. He'll go get us a cooler and some beer and then meet us over on Oak Street. From there, we'll walk down to the bridge and party," Cameron told them.

"Hey, Ben!" Jackie yelled from across the room.

"Hey, Jackie, you ready to have some fun?" Ben asked.

"I was born ready," she said.

Jackie gave Ben a big hug, and Ben was stunned. That wasn't an ordinary hug; it was a hug with a lot more intention behind it. Ben just smiled and looked over at Johnny. Johnny gave a thumbs up and then walked over to where Jessica was.

"There's my brother. You guys give me the rest of the money, and I'll go talk to him," Mark said.

They rounded the money up, and Mark went out to his brother's truck. When Mark and his brother were done talking, his brother pealed out to show off for everyone. Mark waved his hand, and the ten of them left the Hall and were headed to Oak Street.

When they all got down to the bridge, the guys gathered firewood, and the girls sat around talking. Trey had brought a lighter and a small bottle of lighter fluid. He soaked the wood in lighter fluid, and with the spark of the lighter, they had a fire going.

"Let's drink some beer, guys!" Johnny yelled.

The girls started laughing as Johnny and Mark handed out beers.

"Move your arms Ben, I want to sit on your lap" Jackie told him.

"Sit on down baby" Ben replied with a confident attitude from the beer

Jackie was laughing as she sat down, and almost missed his lap. After she got situated on Ben's lap, Ben felt something hit his chest. When he looked down, he saw a condom lying on Jackie's Jacket.

"You might need that Benny boy" Cameron told him

Ben didn't like being called Benny, but he was feeling pretty good and didn't really care at the moment.

"We going to need that Ben" Jackie asked

"We'll just have to see" he replied

Ben then stood up, took Jackie's hand and led her away from the others. After about three minutes of walking through the bushes, Ben then turned towards Jackie stumbling a little from the beer.

Jackie then leaned forward and started kissing Ben. Ben was liking it, and they began to make out. The moment was getting heated, when all of a sudden; Ben had flashes of Stephanie running through his head. Ben still cared for Stephanie, and had pictured this moment with her, not Jackie.

"I can't do this" Ben said as he jumped up

"What's wrong, you scared or something," Jackie asked

"No, Jackie," Ben replied

Ben didn't want them all to make fun of him, so he just started walking toward his bike.

"Fine, don't ever talk to me again" Jackie yelled

Ben got on his bike and took off for home. The whole way home, he thought about Stephanie and wondered what she was doing at that moment. Maybe she was out doing the same kind of thing right then. It's not like she was going to hold out for him. She was over 400 miles away. Still, Ben couldn't understand how a girl who was 400 miles away could have that kind of an effect on him. When he got home, he looked at the clock, and it was only 10 p.m.

His mom was in the living room and jumped up when Ben walked around the corner.

"Hi, Ben. Did you have fun?" she asked.

"Sure, Mom," Ben said. He was still a little tipsy.

"Ben," his mom said as he passed her.

"What, Mom?"

"Is that *beer* on your breath?" she asked.

Ben lowered his head. "Yeah. A few friends and I drank a couple beers—so what?" he said.

"*So what?*" she paused. "You're not old enough to drink beer. But on the other hand, teenagers have been doing it for years, and I figured this day would come eventually."

Ben couldn't believe what his mom had said. He then raised his head to look at her. He knew his mom was cool, but this cool didn't cross his mind.

"You just go on up to your room. I'll make you some food and bring it up to you. Your dad will be home soon, and if we get you into bed, he won't have to know about this," she told him.

"Thanks, Mom. You're the best," he said with a big smile.

Ben stayed home the rest of the weekend to avoid his friends—Jackie, especially. He knew that when Monday came, he would have to face them, but at least he had a couple of days to think about it. He still didn't want to tell Jackie the real reason why he had done what he'd done. He was hoping she would just forgive him with no explanation.

Monday morning, Ben took off for school early to try and avoid Jackie. He was sure this would work, but he was only half right. Johnny knew how Ben's mind worked, so he left early, too, so he could catch him on the way.

"Hey, Ben—wait up," Johnny yelled.

Ben stopped his bike and waited for Johnny. Ben figured if anyone would understand him, it would be Johnny.

"What happened Friday night?" Johnny asked.

"You'd just make fun of me if I told you," Ben told him with a serious look on his face.

"No, I won't," Johnny replied.

"Promise me you won't tell anyone?" Ben said.

"I promise, Ben. You can trust me," he said.

"Everything was going alright right up until I was headed for home plate. At that moment, all I could think about was Stephanie," Ben told him.

"*Stephanie?*" Johnny said in surprise.

"Yeah. I think my heart has already been taken. I don't know if there is anything I can do about it," Ben said.

"Wow, Ben. I didn't know you felt that way about Stephanie," Johnny replied.

"Nobody knows but you. The day Steph left, she made it clear to me that she felt the same way, but I still didn't have the guts to tell her."

As Ben was going to tell Johnny more about it, Jackie was riding around the corner.

"Hey, guys."

"Hey, Jackie," they said at the same time.

"Can I talk to you, Ben? Alone?" Jackie asked as she looked at Johnny.

"I'll see you guys at school," Johnny said.

"Ben, I'm sorry about Friday night. I was feeling pretty good, and I really like you—"

Ben cut her off. "No, Jackie, I'm the one that should apologize. Maybe we can start over and just stay at first base for a while," Ben told her.

"That sounds good, Ben. You want to race to school?" Jackie asked.

"Sure. I'll give you a head start," Ben replied.

Ben was glad it was taken care of before school instead of during school. All of the guys except Johnny would have ragged on him. Ben's day turned out to be good for a Monday.

After school, Ben went to the Hall to hang out. When Ben was at the Hall that late afternoon, he realized that the Hall was his new den. His mind was always at ease there. Ben's dad's company was starting to lose work, and his dad was being more abusive toward his mom.

After a few hours, Ben went on home to see what his mom was doing. When Ben got home, the neighbors were outside on their porch. Mr. and Mrs. Fitch were an older couple that had moved into Stephanie's old house. They seemed like nice people, but they also seemed nosy. They would keep to themselves, though, and were not very talkative. Ben never introduced himself, and he wasn't anxious to do so, either. Ben walked through the front door of his house. His parents were yelling at each other.

"I'm tired of this," he heard his dad say and it was followed by a loud slap.

Ben could hear his mom hit the ground, so he went in to see if she was okay.

"Mom, are you al—" Ben didn't get to finish what he had to say because his dad cut him off.

"Leave her alone, Ben, she's fine," his dad told him.

That's when his mom looked up at Ben. Blood was running down her face.

"Mom, your nose is bleeding," Ben said as anger was building in him.

"I *said* leave her alone, Ben!" his dad yelled.

Ben had had enough of his mom being beaten, and he decided he was going to take a stand for her.

"No, Dad—*you* leave her alone! What has she ever done that she deserves to be hit?" Ben said in a firm voice.

Ben's stand did not last long; his dad hit him with a closed fist on the cheek.

"No, Frank, you leave him out of this!" Ben's mom cried.

"You shut up, !" his dad yelled.

Just then, there was a knock at the door.

"Ben, you get up and get the door. Tell whoever it is to get out of here," his dad told him.

Ben was still in shock; his dad had never laid a hand on him until today. Ben went to the door as he was told. Ben opened the door, and officer Athus was standing there. Officer Athus was the D.A.R.E. officer for the school district, and he had known Ben because of it.

"Ben, is everything alright in there?" he asked.

Ben hesitated. He couldn't believe Officer Athus was at the door.

"Ben, the neighbors said they heard some yelling. Are you guys alright?" Officer Athus was getting anxious.

"Yes sir. My dad dropped a wrench on his toe and was cursing up a storm."

Ben's dad heard him say that and came to the door.

"Officer Athus! How have you been?" his dad said.

Ben's dad lured him to the front yard and talked his way out of the situation. Ben contemplated if he had done the right thing. He knew his dad was getting out of control, but he was worried if he said something his mom might get it even worse.

"Thanks. We'll see you later," Ben's dad said as he closed the door. "You did the right thing, Ben."

The way his dad had said that made Ben realize he did not do the right thing. Ben just didn't want anything else to happen to his mom. He was scared that if he had done the right thing, eventually his dad would have taken it out on his mom.

Ben's high school years were going well except for the problems his dad would cause at home. Jackie and he were getting closer, and they were becoming the couple everyone would talk about. Ben and Stephanie had slowly lost touch with each other. Ben just figured that she had gone on with her life and that he should do the same.

GUT FEELING

The date was May 24, 2002. Ben was sixteen years old, and his sophomore year had come to an end. It was the beginning of summer, and Mark was throwing a big party at his house that night. A lot of people were going to stay the night there, so no one would be driving drunk. Ben wasn't sure if he would partake in the drinking because his dad had bought him an El Camino for his sixteenth birthday.

School had just let out, and teenagers were burning rubber all over the parking lot. Ben was in his car waiting on Jackie so that he could do the same.

"Come on, slow poke," Ben yelled as Jackie was coming down the sidewalk.

"I'm coming, you bug-a-boo!" she yelled back at him.

Jackie jumped in the car, and they headed for the Hall. The owner of the Hall had just purchased the shop next door to him and put in a pizza parlor. A lot of the kids from school practically lived at the Hall. They had their fun with friends and good food next door, so they didn't think there was a reason not to.

"So, we're going to Mark's party tonight, right?" Ben asked Jackie as they were driving down the road.

"Yeah, it sounds like it's going to be a blast," Jackie replied.

"I'm just going to call my mom and tell her what I'm doing so my dad doesn't give me a hard time," Ben said.

"Okay, I'll have to go home for a while, and you can pick me up later," Jackie told him.

"Alright," Ben replied

When they got to the Hall, Ben went next door to get Jackie and himself a slice of pizza. Everyone was out in the parking lot talking about the party.

"The party is gonna be off the hook tonight. You guys don't want to miss it," Mark said with excitement.

"Yeah, and to top it off, my sister's friend plays in a local band, and they're going to be playing out there tonight," Cameron said.

"Cool, man. That sounds awesome," Ben replied.

Mark's parents were out of town, and their house was out in the country, so it was a perfect place for a high school party.

"Ben, will you run me home so I can get ready?" Jackie asked.

"Sure, let's go. I'll be back, guys," Ben said.

"Hurry! I miss you already," Johnny said. They all laughed.

Ben spun out of the parking lot and headed for Jackie's house.

"Give me about an hour and a half, then come back and get me," Jackie told Ben.

"Okay, I'll try and remember that," Ben said.

"You better be back to get me," She said as she slapped him on the arm.

"I will. I was just playing," Ben told her.

They pulled up to Jackie's house, and her dad was on the front porch. Jackie's dad liked Ben; he thought he could do no wrong.

"Hi, Ben. You getting ready for next season yet?" her dad asked.

"I'm always ready, Mr. Conner," Ben replied.

"Atta boy," he said.

"I'll see you in a little bit, Jackie," Ben said.

Ben drove down by his house and noticed his dad wasn't home. He decided to stop and talk to his mom really quickly.

"Mom, where are you?" Ben yelled.

"I'm up here, Ben," she replied.

"Mom, the big party is tonight, so more than likely I'm going to stay there," Ben told her.

"Alright, sweetie. You be careful, and if you've been drinking and then change your mind, you call me," she said.

"I will, Mom. I love you," Ben said.

"I love you, too," she replied.

Ben went to his room to change clothes and then headed out before his dad got home. Ben wasn't getting along with his dad at all. Ben never got over the night his dad had bloodied his mom's nose and then hit him. His dad thought that buying Ben the car would make Ben talk to him again, but he was wrong. Ben said what he had to, but avoided him most of the time.

Ben and Jackie pulled up to the party, and there were cars everywhere. The house was a big two-story with a pool in the backyard. That's where everybody was going when Ben and Jackie stepped out of the car. They could see at least fifty people in that crowd, and nobody knew how many were already out back.

"Ben, Jackie, come on—the band is getting ready to start," Johnny said as he was running and trying not to spill his beer at the same time.

The band was a local rock band called Thrash. They played mostly alternative rock but would slip some oldies in, too. When they went toward the back patio, Mark was out there with Cameron, and they were pouring some beers from the keg.

"Wassup, Ben?" Mark said.

"Ready to party. Wassup with you?" Ben replied.

"Grab a cup and fill 'er up. We'll go down to the mosh pit," Mark told him.

"I'm going to go with the guys for a while," Ben told Jackie.

"Alright, I'm going to find Trish and Jessica. I'll find you later," she replied.

Ben followed the other guys down to the mosh pit, and there was beer flying everywhere. Ben had never been in a mosh pit before, but after a few blows, he learned he had better start giving the blows instead of receiving the blows. After a half hour, Ben was exhausted from mosh-ing. He went toward the house to find Jackie. Jackie was up by the back of the garage getting lit with her friends.

"Hey, baby," Jackie said to Ben as she wrapped her arms around him.

"What're you drinking, girl?" Ben asked.

"Gold Rush. You want some?" she asked.

"Sure, pour it up," he replied.

Ben took a few shots, and then he and Jackie went to dance. As Ben and Jackie danced, Ben could tell by her gestures that this was the night they would slide home. When the song switched over, Ben told Jackie to come with him. He grabbed her hand and led her up the stairs where they found an empty bedroom.

"What you thinking Ben?" Jackie asked while she was giggling.

"What do you think I'm thinking?" Ben replied.

"I think it's about time," she said as she lunged into his arms.

They shut the door to the room, and leaped onto the bed. Ben was getting worked up, and he ignored the thoughts of Stephanie this time. All of a sudden Jackie sat up.

"What's wrong baby?" Ben asked

She just sat there for a minute and didn't say anything. "Jackie—"

It was now obvious what was wrong; Jackie had drunk too much. She cut Ben short when she threw up all over the floor. Ben helped her to the bathroom, and she finished puking her guts out there.

"Jackie, you want something to eat?" Ben asked.

"No, I'm sorry Ben. This was going to be a special night," Jackie said.

"It's alright. You kind of ruined the moment back there," Ben said as he laughed.

"I know that was pretty gross. I'm going to need to clean that up," she said.

"You need me to get you something?" Ben asked.

"Hand me that mouth wash, and then I'm going to lay on the bed," she replied.

"Here you go. I'll be in the bedroom," Ben told her.

Jackie stumbled back into the room and flopped on the bed next to Ben. Ben just wrapped his arms around her, and they ended up falling asleep.

Ben was in a deep sleep when all of a sudden, he sprang up from the bed. He looked at the clock, it was almost two in the morning. Ben then, in a frantic, started to get his shirt and shoes on. All the commotion he made didn't even wake Jackie; she had drank so much and was sleeping heavily. Ben had a bad feeling about his mom, and he knew he had to go check on her.

Ben rushed down the stairs and noticed there were only a few people still partying. As Ben jumped around passed out people to try and make it to the front door, Johnny was still up.

"Ben, what's wrong?" Johnny asked.

"I just need to go home. I'll call you tomorrow," Ben replied.

"Ben, uh, it *is* tomorrow," Johnny said as he laughed.

"Shut up smartass," Ben told him as he shut the door.

Ben made it to his car and fired it up. He then threw it in drive, spun his tires, and raced home. Ben pulled up quietly to his house and rushed to the door. It was locked, so he fumbled through his keys to find the right one. When he got the door open, he crept into the house. He couldn't hear anyone moving around, so he crept toward the living room. Ben didn't see anyone at first, and then his dad came from the kitchen.

"Where've you been, boy?" his dad asked in a drunken voice.

Ben didn't answer him, because just then, he noticed his mom was lying on the floor in front of the couch.

"Mom! Mom!" he yelled.

"She's alright, Ben. Don't you worry. I've been taking care of her," his dad said.

Ben looked back down at his mom, and she still hadn't moved. Ben was thinking the worst. His dad started walking toward him, and Ben stepped back.

"You stay away from me!" Ben yelled at him as he ran up the stairs.

Ben's dad followed him, and Ben started to freak out. Ben had had enough, and was scared for his life. Ben knew where his dad kept a loaded gun; he went to his parent's room. He figured he didn't have enough time to shut the door and lock it, so he went straight for the gun.

"Ben you little, what are you doing?" his dad asked as he came to the door.

Ben was trembling as he turned toward his dad with the gun in his hand.

"You're not going to hurt me or Mom again. I'm tired of it," Ben said as he was fighting back tears.

"Ben, you put that gun down, or I'm going to whoop your hide!" his dad said in a rage.

"No, Dad, you stay away from me!" Ben yelled back at him.

Ben's dad proceeded toward Ben, and Ben kept backing up.

"Ben, I told you to put—"

It was too late; Ben had backed right up into the bed and slipped and fell back onto it. As Ben came crashing down onto the bed, the gun discharged, hitting his dad. The situation was followed by an eerie silence. Ben just lay there as if he was lifeless; he didn't want to look.

Oh, no. Did I kill him? I don't even hear him moving, Ben thought to himself.

"Ben? Oh, no, Ben—what did you do?" his mom cried.

Ben sat up when he heard his mom's voice. He just sat there and couldn't even speak. His mom was sitting on the floor by the door, bawling her eyes out. Ben couldn't believe what had happened, and his body had gone numb. His mom got up and embraced Ben, holding him tighter than she had ever done before. Ben was in such shock that he hadn't even shed a tear yet.

About fifteen minutes later, Ben could hear the sirens and see the lights flashing through the windows. Ben just sat there staring at his dad's lifeless body. The gun was lying right next to Ben when he heard Officer Athus's voice.

"Ben, don't touch that gun, son," Athus told him.

Ben had no intention of touching that gun again. Officer Athus grabbed the gun and set it on the dresser next to the bed. Ben's mom was crying so hard she couldn't even open her eyes. Officer Athus saw the bruises on Ben's mom's face. He knew that this had to be an accident, but Ben's mom's face hadn't. At that point, Officer Athus wished he would have done more investigating in the past so that this night would never have happened.

Word spread quickly, and by noon the next day, the whole town knew what had happened. Of course the story had changed several times. Most people wouldn't know the real story until the trial, so it would be the talk of the town for quite a while. Ben's mom went out the next day and got him a good lawyer. She was hoping Ben would get very little consequence for what happened. Her little Ben was in a big mess, but she knew it would all work out. No matter what anyone would say about it, she knew Ben didn't mean for that to happen.

THE TRUTH

Ben was being held in juvenile detention and was isolated from the other kids. The courts wanted him to be evaluated to make sure he wasn't a threat to the other kids. Ben was still in disbelief over the whole situation. When reality set in, he couldn't eat, sleep, and didn't even want to talk to anyone. There was one thing that stood out in Ben's mind, though. Ben knew his mom could never be beaten again. He still didn't understand where all the anger that his dad had had for his mom had come from.

Three days passed like a blur. On the fourth day, Ben started to eat again and was given his first evaluation. Ben opened up to the psychologist and told him everything. Ben told him how his dad was always angry with his mom, and he didn't understand why. He told him how it got worse over the years, and how he would find different places to go that made him comfortable. He also told him that that night was an accident, and he was scared that his mom was dead. Ben broke down crying because of all the things they were talking about.

At the end of the meeting, Ben told him he would take it back if he were able. He was just trying to protect his mom; he had thought he could scare his dad away with the gun. He said that when he slipped and the gun went off, he went in to a whole new world.

The psychologist took everything Ben had told him into consideration and came to the conclusion that Ben was a victim of mental abuse. She told the court that he was not a troubled boy; he had just made a bad choice. Ben's dad had been physically abusive toward his mom, but not really to Ben. Ben was just damaged in that he cared so much for his mom. When his dad would abuse his mom, he was mentally abusing Ben and didn't realize it. He told them he would need some therapy, but he was not a threat to anyone. When Ben's mom heard the results of the evaluation, she was thrilled for Ben. This meant that he had a really good shot at some sympathy from the court.

On the seventh day, Ben's mom was able to visit him. Ben got two hours to visit with his mom, and she was there for every second.

"Ben, I'm so sorry this all happened. I should have gotten you out of there a long time ago," she told him.

"Mom, it wasn't me he was hitting all the time, it was you," Ben replied.

"I know, sweetie, I just—" Ben cut her off.

"Mom, don't beat yourself up over it. He could have killed you that night. He's gone now, and we don't have to make excuses for him anymore. You never deserved all of the bad things he did to you. Now you're safe, and I'll be okay, Mom; we don't have to worry," Ben told her.

The roles had changed for once. Ben was finding all the positive things to say at such a bad moment; that was usually his mom's job.

"How did you get to be so strong?" she asked as she was tearing up.

"I got this way because of you, Mom," he replied.

She then began crying more and embraced Ben as if she would never let him go. After they cried together, Ben's mom had something to tell him.

"The lawyer says it's looking really good," his mom said.

"How long will I be in here, Mom?" he asked.

"The lawyer says he can probably get you released when you are eighteen," she said.

"Eighteen..." Ben said as he shook his head. "Well, I guess it could be a lot worse."

When the visit was all over, Ben had to go back to the bunks. There was a kid that tried giving Ben a hard time, but Ben would just ignore him. Ben didn't want to get in anymore trouble, and he knew that if he let that kid get to him, he would. Ben just went to his bed and thought about what all his friends were probably thinking about him.

They've got to know the truth by now, I hope, he thought to himself. As Ben lay there, he thought about all the positive things in his life. He also thought about how he wished his dad had been there more for him. Now it was too late, and Ben would never know whether his dad could have changed.

Ben was getting anxious waiting for the next court date. Meanwhile, there was one kid that Ben was able to talk to. Chris Hopkins was being held for a robbery he and his friends had committed. Chris tagged along one day with his friends, and they decided it would be cool to make some money by robbing a house they knew had money. The one thing they didn't plan on was for the people to be home. The owner of the home heard the commotion and went to his living room with a gun. The three kids, including Chris, darted back out the window. Chris and his friends were apprehended an hour later. Chris regretted being there, and would tell Ben all about it.

Chris helped keep Ben positive, too. Some days, Ben was so down he wouldn't want to talk. All it took was Chris to make him laugh a few times, and Ben was talking again. Chris was the only kid in there that Ben had told what had happened that night. Chris couldn't believe what he heard at first, but sympathized for Ben. He told Ben about the judge Ben would be in front of, and that the judge was beaten when *he* was a kid.

"Judge Harris is his name, Ben," Chris said.

"He was beaten when he was a kid?" Ben asked.

"Yeah, and he will probably have a great deal of sympathy for you. It's not like you meant for that to happen, and you were just protecting your mom," Chris told him.

"I hope you're right," Ben replied.

"I'm pretty sure you won't be in here past eighteen," Chris said.

Ben went back to his bed that night and thought about what he and Chris had talked about. Ben really hoped Chris was right about the judge and him being lenient. Ben still knew that only time would tell, and he was trying not to worry about it too much.

A couple months went by before the next court date, and Ben was getting really anxious. The morning of the court date, Ben got up early to get ready to meet his mom and the lawyer before court.

"Ben, we got a plea agreement offer, do you want to hear what they had to say?" His lawyer asked.

"Yes. I've been ready," Ben replied.

"The district attorney thinks you should stay in state custody. They want to help you with any issues you may have from this. You'll get to finish high school and pick a field of work so you can get a job when you turn eighteen. Then, when your schooling is done and you turn eighteen, they will do another psychological exam. When they see you're not a threat to society, you will be released and ready to take on the world. So, what do you think, guys?"

Ben just sat there for a minute to soak it all up. Ben's mom gave him a hug and knew Ben really wanted to come home.

"I guess that would be the best thing for me at this moment. I mean, it did happen, and even though it was an accident, I know there have to be some kind of consequences," Ben told them.

"I think you'll be fine, Ben. You're a strong boy, and I know you'll make it through this," his mom told him as she was about to cry.

"Thanks, Mom. I know you'll be there keeping me strong," Ben said.

"I'll be there 'til the end," she replied.

They signed the plea agreement, and Ben began doing what he had to do to fulfill his part of the deal. Chris was only fifteen, and he only had to stay a year in state custody. He and Ben kept each other focused on what they had to do.

The day Chris left, Ben still had nine months left until he turned eighteen. Ben just kept to himself after Chris left because he didn't care for the other kids there. All the other kids were troublemakers, and some of them were going to adult detention after that.

Ben went on with his business and studied hard so he could get his schooling done early. He got his GED and was two months away from graduating his heavy equipment certification. Ben was always fascinated with the big equipment on construction sites. When he had the chance to be certified to run them, he jumped right on the opportunity. Ben had become very mature for his age, and was feeling good about himself.

The date was April 24, 2004. Ben's birthday was in a few weeks, and he was getting very excited about it. He was ready to be free and ready to see his friends again. The thing he wanted the most, though, was to be with his mom. That day was visitation day, and Ben was waiting for his mom to show up. She was a little later than usual, but she still made it, as always.

"Hi, Mom. I've missed you," Ben said.

"I've missed you, too, honey," she replied.

Ben could tell that there was something wrong with his mom. She had learned to hide things from Ben a little better over the years, but Ben could still see right through her.

"What's wrong, Mom?" Ben asked.

"Ben, we need to talk. Let's go find a place to sit down," she told him.

The facility had a garden area that was enclosed, and they could visit with family out there. That's where Ben and his mom found a bench to sit—right beside a big rose bush. Ben's mom was really worried about what she had to tell him, but she figured she'd just get right to the point.

"Ben, I've been diagnosed with leukemia. They found it about three weeks ago," she said.

Ben's jaw hit the ground, and he was speechless. The last person he had left in this world was telling him she might not be there much longer. He didn't know what to say.

"Ben, I got some results back this week. They say with the right treatment I can beat this thing," she told him.

Ben lost it, and started to cry.

"Ben, stay strong because I have to tell you more," she said as she fought back tears.

Ben looked at her with disbelief. What else could there be?

"Ben, there are things from the past that you don't know about. First, I want you to know that I love you more than anything in this world," she told him.

"I know, Mom. I've always known," he replied.

"Ben, I'm not your real mother."

Ben thought she was joking at first, but then he realized that she had on her serious face.

"Your mom died giving birth to you. Your dad was sitting there after you were born, waiting for her to wake up. She flat-lined, and they tried to get her heart beating again but were unsuccessful. She had internal bleeding that they didn't catch, and her heart gave out."

By this time in the conversation, Ben was blown away. The woman he had called "Mom" all these years and loved more than the world wasn't even his real mom.

"Ben, if you don't want to call me 'Mother' anymore, I understand. I was never supposed to tell you this, but I can't hold it in any longer. If I were to leave this world, I would roll in my grave if I didn't tell you this. My name is Anna Cassel, formerly Anna Jasper. Your dad and I got married six months after you were born. I could never have kids, and your dad was very hurt over your mom. He thought that was the solution, obviously, to marry me. With me not being able to have kids, he wouldn't ever have to go through that kind of pain again. Your dad just wanted a woman to take care of you, and I don't think he ever truly loved me. I fell in love with you, though, and I'm proud to call you my son. You look so much like your mother, and I think that is why your dad never took the time to get close to you. He loved your mother so much. He never got over her death."

"Do you have pictures of her?" Ben asked.

"Yes, Ben, I have a whole chest full of stuff for you," his mom replied with a smile.

Ben was really shocked, but he did not feel mad over what she had told him. He was glad she told him, and as far as he was concerned, she was still "Mom."

"You're still my mom. I might have had a biological mom, but it is what it is. You raised me, and I love you for being here my whole life," he told her.

His mom then cried tears of joy. She was so glad he did not hate her for what she was forced to hide.

"Ben, there is one last thing, and it is good news," she said.

"What, Mom?" he replied.

"Back when you were eight, I took ten thousand dollars and invested it in stocks for you. Let's just say that you're up to about three hundred thousand, and when you turn eighteen, it is all yours," she said with a smile.

"Are you serious?" Ben was ecstatic.

"You make sure you're smart with all that money," she added.

Ben had soaked up everything his mom had told him that day. He was happy she never gave up on him and that she loved him like he was hers. Ben was missing his friends, though, due to them not being able to see him the whole time. The only person that was allowed to visit was his mom. She was the only family he had left besides some cousins he didn't even know.

Jackie had moved to California and couldn't fathom the thought of telling Ben. A couple of weeks before he was supposed to get out, Johnny broke the news about Jackie to Ben in a letter he wrote. It didn't even bother Ben; he'd felt their relationship would be short term, anyway. Ben knew he would be lucky to ever find someone like Stephanie again.

LIFE'S CIRCLE

Ben got his mind focused those last few weeks, despite all the things he was told. He focused on getting a job when he got out. The facility let him put in applications on the internet because they knew he would be getting released. Ben was great the whole time and at the end, he was helping other kids get motivated to change their lives for the better.

The week after Ben's birthday, his paperwork was complete and he was released. Anna, who was still "Mom" to Ben, was there anticipating Ben's release. She was ready to take him home. As Ben came through those doors to freedom, he and Anna embraced.

"Thanks for being here, Mom," he said.

"You know I would not have missed this for the world, sweetie. Now, let's go home," she replied.

As they were pulling into the driveway of their home, Johnny was pulling up in front of the house. Johnny had a new Mustang, and he had Cameron and Trey with him.

"Ben, you're alive!" Cameron yelled.

"What did you do, hit the weights, or what?" Johnny asked.

Ben was in pretty good shape when he got out. When he would get done with all his work, he would exercise to kill time.

"How've you guys been?" asked Ben.

"We're graduating. Wishing you were there," Trey said.

"Yeah, school and sports just wasn't the same without you," Jonny told him.

"Come on, Ben, let's go down to the Hall and you can see the others," Cameron said.

"No, thanks. I'm just going to spend time with my mom," he replied.

"Alright, mama's boy. Just kidding, Ben. We'll catch up with you later," Cameron told him.

Cameron and Trey went back to the car, and Johnny walked up to Ben and gave him a big hug.

"I know you've been through a lot, Ben. I'm glad we became friends, and I'll always be there for you, man," Johnny told him.

"I know. You're the only friend that wrote all the way up to the end. Thanks, man—it kept my spirits up." Ben replied.

"Call me later if you want to do something," Johnny said.

"Alright. I will, Johnny. See you later," Ben told him as he gave him a pat on the back.

When Ben walked into the house, he got an eerie feeling. Anna could tell that it was rough for him to walk into that house after what had happened there. She was waiting to do anything with the house until Ben got released from custody.

"Ben, are you alright?" she asked.

"Yeah. It's just different now. Even though Dad is gone, I can still feel his presence." Ben told her.

"Ben, we don't have to stay here. I just stayed to be close to you, and you can decide if you want to move. Right now, though, you need to come with me," she told him.

Anna took Ben up to the attic where she had kept the chest that had his mom and dad's things in it.

"There it is, Ben. These are things your dad kept. Most of it is your mom's, and I put a few of your dad's things in it, too," Anna told him.

Ben opened it up as if there were treasure inside. Anna could tell he was excited and eager to see what was inside. The first thing Ben saw was his mom's wedding dress she had worn when his parents got married. Beside the dress was a picture from their wedding day, and Ben's dad had the biggest smile he had ever seen. Ben couldn't recall his dad ever having smiled that big in his life. Under the dress was a picture of a man he had never seen before.

"Who is this?" Ben asked.

"That was your grandpa. Your mother's dad's name was Ben, too. He passed away while your mom was in college. She wanted to name you after him, but they were still undecided the day she had you. Your dad said the name Ben would suit you, but he never got the chance to tell her. Your dad knew she was watching, though, and he made sure her wish was fulfilled," she told him.

"Wow, I'm named after my grandpa. I always wondered whom I got my name from," he replied.

Ben had always thought of Anna's parents as his grandparents, but they, too, were only pictures. Her parents had also passed away when she was young. Ben kept going through the things and finding a lot of pictures of his mom and dad together. They both seemed so happy in those pictures, and their smiles made Ben tear up.

"Why didn't he care?" Ben asked.

"Oh, honey, he cared more than you know. It tore him up inside, and he never talked about it. Instead, he took it out on me." She paused. "Ben, he is with her now, and I think he's finally happy again," she told him.

"You're right. I've seen enough for now," Ben said as he shut the chest.

"Come on, sweetie, I'll make you some spaghetti and meatballs. How's that sound?" she said with a smile.

Ben then smiled for the first time since being back in the house.

"You still know how to make me smile, Mom," he replied.

That night, Ben was restless most of the night. When he did finally doze off to sleep, he had a dream about his dad.

"Son, wake up," his dad said.

"Dad, is that you?" Ben asked.

"I'm in spirit, Ben. I'm at peace, Ben, and I don't want you to be sorry for what happened. You were a good boy, and will be an even better man. I'm here with your mom, and we're both proud of you. Move out of this house, and move on with your life," his dad told him.

Ben jumped up out of bed and looked around for his dad. It felt as if his dad were just there. When he got his bearings back, he dozed back off to sleep. In the morning, Ben remembered everything from his dream and told Anna about it.

"Well, start looking for a house you like, and then we'll sell this one," she told him.

"Alright. Sounds good to me," he replied.

One of the local construction companies called Ben in for an interview. The guy that interviewed him liked him so much that he hired him on the spot. Ben was excited about his new job and liked the pay he would be getting, thanks to his certificate. During the next few weeks, he spent all his extra time looking for the right house. Ben told Anna he still wanted her to live with him. He was going to take care of her since she had always been there for him. Ben and Anna found a house they both loved. It was built on a couple acres and looked out over a pond. Once they had finished all the paperwork, they started packing.

Ben was getting his things packed in his room one day when the doorbell rang.

"Ben, come down here. Someone is here to see you!" Anna yelled.

Ben figured it was Johnny because Johnny had told him he would help him this weekend.

"Tell him to come up!" Ben yelled back.

Ben heard the footsteps coming up the stairs; they didn't sound like Johnny's footsteps. When Ben lifted his head, he couldn't believe who was standing there.

"Steph, is that you?" Ben said in disbelief.

"Yes, Ben, it's me," she replied with a grin.

Ben was looking at a Stephanie that was no longer a girl. She was a young, beautiful woman. She had beautiful blonde hair and her bright green eyes were glowing. *Stephanie has filled out nicely*, Ben thought to himself. Stephanie had come around more slowly than most girls, but caught up just fine. Ben then went over and gave her a big hug.

"Where did you come from?" he asked.

"Dallas. When I turned eighteen, I decided I was coming back to look you up," she said.

"I'm so glad to see you, Steph. I've had a couple of rough years," Ben told her.

"I know. I talked to Johnny. I stopped by a couple of days ago, but you guys were not home," she said.

"So, how has your life been going?" he asked.

"I've been alright. My dad is overly protective, as always. When I told him I wanted to come look you up, though, he thought it would be good for me. He could tell I was very sad when we left. Ben, I tried to move on and meet other people, but no one compared to you. Ben, I want to be here for you," she told him as she held his hand.

"So, you don't have someone back there waiting on you?" Ben asked.

"No, the one I wanted has been here the whole time," Stephanie told him as she looked into his eyes.

Ben then knew he wasn't going to let her go again. He embraced her and kissed her like he wished he had done a long time ago. As he ran his fingers up the back of her neck and into her hair, his fingers got caught in her necklace. He slowly pulled out the necklace, hoping it was what he thought it was. He was right; it was the "Best Friends Forever" necklace he had given her on her tenth birthday. Ben then unbuttoned his shirt, and there was his.

"You kept it," she said.

"Yeah, of course. I see you did the same. I thought you would lose it after we lost touch," Ben told her.

"No. I've known where my heart has been for a long time," she replied with a smile.

"I've felt this way for a long time, too. I just didn't want to tell you when we were younger. I loved the fact that you were my friend, and I didn't want that fact to change," Ben replied.

"Oh, Ben, you never would have lost me," she said.

Ben and Stephanie were reunited again, and it was as if they had never parted. The intimate parts were a little different for them, but they were like a hammer and nails—meant for each other.

Stephanie moved back for good, and a year later, they were married. Ben's new house was more than big enough to accommodate the three of them. Ben, Stephanie, and Anna were happier than they had ever been before. There was also a little one on the way, and Anna couldn't wait to be a grandma. Anna's therapy had worked; the leukemia was gone, and Ben was happy she would be around for years to come.

The only two women Ben loved more than anything would be there to share his new den with him. Ben now knew that all the things that happened to him had reasons behind them, and he was a stronger person because of them. Ben would think of his parents from time to time. He knew they were looking down on him and that they were proud of him.

Anna had sold his dad's company and put the money up for Ben's family. She knew Ben would take care of her, and maybe one day, she might find herself a mister right. Until that day, though, she was content being there for Ben and Stephanie in any way she could.

Johnny would still stop by from time to time to see how things were going. Ben was happy that Johnny turned out to be such a good friend. That was a good example of how the only thing he could count on in life was everything changes. From Jake, to Kirk, to all the other things that took place, some were good and some bad. Ben was glad his mom taught him to be so positive, and he knew that that positivity is what had helped him through most of it.

As for Ben and Stephanie, they were madly in love, and nothing could change that. Ben was certain of one thing for sure: Ben's den was complete, and he knew it would be anywhere his family was until the day he left this ever-changing world.

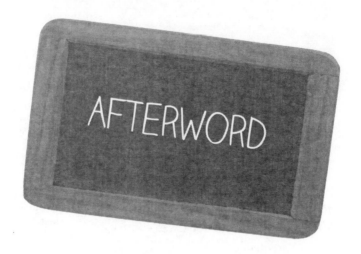

AFTERWORD

I hope you liked my first book, and there will be many more to come. Look for my next book, *Purple Ghosts*, and if you liked this one, then you'll love that one. Best wishes to whomever reads my books and also those that don't, and remember:

> Positive things will always prevail as long as we never give up on positivity.

Hope you enjoy the Story!

Edward Terrell Sr.

8-9-2012